LYNCHING
of
Louie Sam

a novel by

ELIZABETH STEWART

annick press
toronto + new york + vancouver

Annick Press Ltd.

Edited by Pam Robertson
Copyedited by Linda Pruessen
Cover design by Natalie Olsen, Kisscut Design
Cover background image © lama-photography / photocase.com

We acknowledge the support of the Canada Council for the Arts, the Ontario Arts Council, and the Government of Canada through the Canada Book Fund (CBF) for our publishing activities.

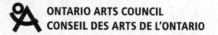

**ONTARIO ARTS COUNCIL
CONSEIL DES ARTS DE L'ONTARIO**

Cataloging in Publication

Stewart, Elizabeth (Elizabeth Mary)
    The lynching of Louie Sam / Elizabeth Stewart.

ISBN 978-1-55451-439-7 (bound).—ISBN 978-1-55451-438-0 (pbk.)

    1. Sam, Louie, d. 1884—Juvenile fiction. 2. British Columbia—
History—1871-1918—Juvenile fiction. I. Title.

PS8637.T49445L96 2012   jC813'.6   C2012-901957-7

Distributed in Canada by:
Firefly Books Ltd.
66 Leek Crescent
Richmond Hill, ON
L4B 1H1

Published in the U.S.A. by
Annick Press (U.S.) Ltd.
Distributed in the U.S.A. by:
Firefly Books (U.S.) Inc.
P.O. Box 1338
Ellicott Station
Buffalo, NY 14205

MIX
Paper from
responsible sources
FSC® C004071
www.fsc.org

ANCIENT FOREST ™
FRIENDLY

Printed in Canada
Visit us at: www.annickpress.com

On the night of February 27, 1884, two white teenagers followed a lynch mob comprised of their fathers and almost a hundred other American settlers north from the Washington Territory into British Columbia, Canada. There they seized Louie Sam, a member of the Stó:lō First Nation, from lawful custody and hung him, claiming he was guilty of murdering one of their own. This novel is the fictionalized story of those two teenagers, George Gillies and Peter Harkness. Readers should be advised that the racism expressed by these and other characters, while offensive, is meant to reflect the attitudes of the period.

I have taken care in writing this historical fiction not to presume to express the thoughts or feelings of Louie Sam or the Stó:lō people, apart from what has been reported in the public record. The story of Louie Sam—who he was and what the injustice of his death meant and continues to mean to the Stó:lō Nation—remains to be told.

According to the Tuskegee Institute of Alabama, between 1882 and 1968 there were 4,742 lynchings in the United States. In Canada during the same period there was one— the lynching of Louie Sam.

"Groups tend to be more immoral than individuals."
—Martin Luther King Junior

FOR LOUIE SAM

CHAPTER ONE

Washington Territory, 1884

MY NAME IS GEORGE GILLIES. My parents are Scottish by birth and I was born in England, but since we immigrated, we're all Americans now. We live near the town of Nooksack in the Washington Territory, just south of the International Border with British Columbia, Canada. Mam says the way we children speak, we sound just like we were born here.

In Scotland and England, my father, Peter Gillies, worked the farmlands of one rich laird after another. He likes to tell anyone who will listen that we came to America for freedom's sake—by which, he'll add with a wink, he means the land he purchased almost for free from lumbermen here in the Nooksack Valley. Father considered it a bargain because the land had already been cleared of the giant fir trees that grow in these parts to a hundred feet or more. Our house is a log cabin made from those firs, but we have plans to build a fine two-story plank house one day.

Father likes his joke, but he is serious about freedom, too. He tells us kids never to forget that the land we own is ours for all time and makes us free in ways we never could have been in Great Britain. Here, Father answers to no one but himself and God. And Mam says he only answers to God on Sundays.

A couple of years back, my brothers and I helped Father build a dam on Sumas Creek, which cuts through our land. We run a gristmill off the millpond that resulted from that dam. Homesteaders bring wagonloads of grain and corn from miles around to our mill to be ground into flour and meal. The driveshaft is trimmed from a Lodgepole pine and the waterwheel and pit wheel are made from fir. Father has plans to bring in a steel driveshaft from back east once the Canadians finish building their railroad through British Columbia. And once we've saved enough money from selling our miller's toll—the portion of flour that Father keeps as payment.

Between the mill and the farm, we work hard from dawn to dusk. Father says that's the price of freedom. Me, I count myself lucky that even if I wasn't born free, I am free now. Out here in the frontier a man can be whoever he sets his mind to be. My friend Pete Harkness was born in the States—Minnesota, to be exact—and he never lets me forget it.

"You'll never be president," Pete is fond of telling me.

He's referring to the fact that the United States Constitution requires that presidents be born on American soil—as though Pete, who had to repeat tenth grade, thinks that being born here makes him better fit for the job than I am. Pete and I are in the same grade now, but he's sixteen and reminds me every chance he gets that he's a year older than I am. Mam says not to mind him, that Pete hasn't had the advantage of being raised in a God-fearing family the way I have, at least not since his mother died three years ago and his father took up with Mrs. Bell. I have never heard Mam gossip about Mrs. Bell the way some people do, but I can tell from the way Mam's lips go tight at the mention of her name that she disapproves of her.

THIS SUNDAY PAST, you could say fate took me by the hand. I was walking my brothers and sister the four miles from our property to Sunday school at the Presbyterian church in Nooksack when halfway there we saw smoke rising above the trees. That in itself wasn't unusual—on a February morning, you'd be worried if you *didn't* see smoke rising from a chimney. But this was different: thick and black.

"That's coming from Mr. Bell's cabin," said John.

The Mr. Bell he was referring to was James Bell, an old-timer who ran a store out of his cabin, selling a few supplies to get by. He was also the lawful husband of the very same Mrs. Bell who is currently living under the roof of my friend Pete's father.

We hurried around the bend in the trail ahead to see what was the cause of the smoke. Flames were leaping above the trees by the time we started down the narrow path through a thicket of dogwood that led from the trail to the cabin. When we got to the clearing, the wood shack was going up like tinder. Fire was licking out of the windows of the front room, where Mr. Bell kept his dry goods for sale. If I'd let him, John—who is thirteen and a know-it-all—would have rushed right up to it. Will, a year younger than John and pretty much John's shadow, would have been right behind him.

"Mr. Bell?" I called from a safe distance, holding John and Will back.

There was no answer, just the loud crack of blistering wood. I thought about running to the closest farmstead for help, the Breckenridges', but it would have been a good twenty minutes to get there, and another twenty back.

I tried again. "Mr. Bell!"

"He can't hear you!" said John.

I had to admit John was right. The bursting and crackling of the fire was making too much noise. There was nothing to do but inch up and have a look inside that inferno.

"You stay here with Annie," I told Will. Annie is

only nine, and I could see her eyes were wide with fright.

John and I crept alongside the cabin toward the back, where the flames hadn't caught hold yet, shielding ourselves from the heat. We peered through a window and saw Mr. Bell lying face down on the floor between the storeroom and the kitchen at the rear. A fog of smoke was quickly filling the space above him.

"We got to get him out!" declared John.

"Let's hope he's got a back door," I yelled over the din, because it was obvious we were not going through the front way.

We ran to the rear of the cabin and were relieved to see that there was a way into his kitchen. When we pushed open the door, smoke came rushing out at us. It stung our eyes and blinded us, but after a moment it cleared enough for us to see Mr. Bell lying there.

"Mr. Bell!" I called again, but he wasn't budging.

The fire was traveling fast from the front room. We had to get him out of there.

"Hold your breath!" I shouted to John.

The two of us dashed inside. I suppose it paid to be brothers that day, because without having to plan it, we each grabbed hold of one of Mr. Bell's arms and dragged him out of there, like his limbs were branches on a log we were lugging to reinforce our dam. He was heavy enough that even with two of us we made slow progress toward the back door. A loud bang from the front room sent the taste of fear up from my stomach into my throat. I looked up to see burning timbers falling, and daylight where the roof used to be. I glanced at John. If he was as scared as I was, he didn't let it show. He just kept hauling Mr. Bell toward the door. I did what he did. Pretty soon we had Mr. Bell out on the grass and we were filling our lungs with good air.

John was a sight—his face streaked with grime, his Sunday clothes covered in ash and soot—and I reckon I was, too. My first thought was that Mam would have our hides for ruining our Sunday best. But that thought was chased from my head when I looked down at Mr. Bell. He still hadn't moved, and at a glance I saw the reason why—the back of his head was nothing but a bloody mess. John had gone pale. Annie and Will stood staring. Me, I felt my stomach rising. I'd chopped the head off many a chicken and watched the blood spurt, but this was different.

"What happened to him?" Annie asked, her voice high and frightened.

"Is he dead?" asked Will.

I knelt down and rolled him over. His eyes were wide open. His skin was gray against the white of his beard, and I could count what teeth he had left through his gaping mouth. The first thought that came into my head was,

"We got to fetch Doctor Thompson."

"What the hell for?" John huffed. "Can't you see he's a goner?!"

"Don't be cursing in front of Annie," I told him.

"He looks surprised," she said.

"You'd be surprised, too, if your head got bashed in," said John.

"How do you reckon it happened?" asked Will.

The three of them were looking down at Mr. Bell with unseemly curiosity, considering how recently his spirit had departed this world. I found a horse blanket on the woodpile and threw it over him.

"It's not for us to say," I told them. "We need to fetch the sheriff."

CHAPTER TWO

MR. BELL'S CABIN WAS A COUPLE OF MILES from Nooksack. John and I argued about which one of us should go for Sheriff Leckie to tell him about the violent end that had befallen Mr. Bell, and which one should stay with Annie, who had begun to blub and complain at the prospect of being left behind with a dead body.

"Stop crying," John told her. "Nobody even liked the old coot."

"Leave her be," I said.

Annie buried her head in my chest, adding tears and snot to the streaks of grime on my jacket—and settling which one of us would be dispatched for the sheriff to deliver the biggest news that had ever happened in the Nooksack Valley.

"All right, you go," I told John. "Take Will with you. And run."

"I know to run!" John snarled back, needing the last word just like always.

The four of us walked together down the path

to the trail. Annie and I watched our brothers take off at top speed toward town until they were out of sight. Now that she was a sufficient distance from the burning cabin—and from the body lying under the blanket—Annie calmed down.

"We should go home," she said. "We should tell Father what happened."

Mam is expecting a new baby any minute, and Father had stayed home from church to help mind Isabel, who's three. Father isn't big on churchgoing and preachers, anyway. He says he doesn't need a middleman between him and the Almighty. He's independent minded, and that's what attracted him to living in America in the first place. Mam's the one who makes us kids go to Sunday school. And she says that since we made the move to the Washington Territory, Father's taken up a little too much frontier spirit for his own good.

"We should wait here," I told Annie. "We found the body. We're witnesses. Sheriff Leckie's going to want to talk to us."

"John can tell him as good as you can."

So now my little sister was arguing with me, too. I was beginning to think I did not command adequate respect from my juniors.

"You stay here," I said, indicating a tree stump where she could sit down.

"Where are you going?"

"To investigate."

"Investigate what?"

"To investigate what happened to poor Mr. Bell."

"John says nobody liked him."

"Just because a man isn't liked doesn't mean he deserved to die."

People say Mr. Bell was strange in the head, starting with the fact that he chose for some reason to build his shack on the edge of a swamp instead of on decent farmland. Maybe that's why Mrs. Bell took their son, Jimmy, and left him. That, and because she's half the old man's age.

"Why would he deserve to die?"

"I just said he didn't!"

"You made it sound like somebody thought he did."

"Just sit there!" I ordered, and walked away into the dogwood patch before she could squabble any further.

When I came out into the clearing, the heat from the cabin was enough to singe my hair. I gave the building a wide berth as I walked around it. The flames had pretty much eaten up the cabin inside and out and were making the leap to an open shed out back. I thought briefly about trying to save a wagon that was parked inside that shed, but the fire was moving too fast and with too much fury. As I watched the roof of the shed fall into the wagon's bed, it dawned on me: Where was Mr. Bell's horse?

"Get away from there!"

I spun around to see Mr. Osterman standing where the path opens from the dogwood into the clearing, motioning at me with his arm. Annie was standing beside him. Bill Osterman is the telegraph man for Nooksack. He is often to be seen riding the trail, checking the telegraph lines that follow it. He's barely thirty, but he's much respected hereabouts, for it's the telegraph that keeps us settlers connected with the states back east, and California to the south. I've often thought that one day I would like to be a telegraph man, like him, living in a nice house in town and not having to wake up with the cows.

"Come away from there, boy!" he yelled. "You'll be burnt as well as roasted!"

I obeyed him.

"We found Mr. Bell!" I told him, coming toward him. To my surprise, my voice cracked as I said it and my throat felt tight—as if any minute I might cry like a girl. I turned away from him while I got hold of myself, pointing to the blanket-covered body lying in the grass. "He's there."

Mr. Osterman went over and raised the blanket only long enough to take in the situation before dropping it and backing away. He's a smart dresser compared to the farm men—maybe he didn't want to get his nice clothes dirty.

"You found him like this?" he asked. His face

looked grim.

"He was inside the cabin. My brother John and I pulled him out."

"And who might you be?"

"George Gillies, sir."

He glanced over at Annie.

"You Peter Gillies's kids?"

"Yes, sir. We were on our way to church. John and Will went ahead to fetch Sheriff Leckie."

He nodded. Then, "Church will still be there next Sunday. You should take your sister on home now, son. This isn't a sight for a little girl."

Part of me knew he was right, but a bigger part of me wanted to stay put. I told him, "I have to wait for my brothers."

"I'll wait here for them to come back with the sheriff, and I'll send them home after you."

"I'd prefer to wait, if you don't mind."

I don't know where I found the gumption. Mr. Osterman stared at me in surprise for a long moment. I thought he was angry, but then he let out a laugh.

"Well, Master Gillies, I can see you are a man who knows his own mind." Then he became serious again.. "Take your sister out by the trail, George. Give me a holler when you see the sheriff coming."

I knew better than to argue with him any further. But I believed it was my duty to inform him, "His horse is gone."

Mr. Osterman looked about Mr. Bell's narrow strip of land, at the small paddock squeezed between the dogwood and the swamp.

"So it is. Likely stolen by whoever did this to him," he said.

"You think somebody killed him?" He didn't seem to hear me.

"Go on now," he said. "Look after your sister."

Annie and I waited by the trail like Mr. Osterman said. I kept my eyes fixed on the point where the trail disappeared into the woods ahead for the first sign of the sheriff. It was a mild day. The sun shone warm on my head. As the roar of the fire simmered down to the odd crackle, you could almost forget that something horrible had happened. But a picture of Mr. Bell's smashed-in head flashed into my mind.

Whoever did this to him, Mr. Osterman had said.

Was he saying somebody had murdered Mr. Bell? If that was the case, the murderer could not be far away. It gave me the shivers just thinking about it, and made me keep a closer eye on Annie.

SHERIFF LECKIE ARRIVED ON horseback a half hour later, without John and Will. The boys were following on foot. He had with him Bill Moultray, who runs the general store and livery stable at The Crossing, a shallow point in the Nooksack River where the Harkness ferry carries folks across. In a way, Mr.

Bell was in competition with Mr. Moultray, selling provisions to the settlers, but Mr. Bell was like fly speck compared to Mr. Moultray, whose business is much bigger—supplying freight teams on the Whatcom Trail, the old gold rush route from the fifties that leads from the Washington Territory up to the Fraser River on the Canadian side of the International Border. Mr. Moultray is a big bug hereabouts, not just because he's rich, but also because he's been to Olympia many times, hobnobbing with the governor and the like.

When I saw the pair of them coming, I ran to fetch Mr. Osterman as he had bid me to do. I found him using a long stick to pick through the hot embers that were pretty near all that was left of Mr. Bell's cabin.

"It's the sheriff!" I called.

He swung around to me fast as could be with a startled look on his face.

"Didn't your pa ever teach you not to sneak up on a person?" he said.

By the time I got done apologizing and the two of us had walked back through the thicket to the trail, the sheriff and Mr. Moultray were pulling up their horses. Mr. Moultray is my father's age, not young and handsome like Mr. Osterman, but he dresses even finer—never to be seen without his gold watch hanging from his waistcoat. Beside Mr. Moultray and Mr. Osterman, Sheriff Leckie looked like a character out of the Buffalo Bill's Wild West show in his dusty hat and long coat. He talks as slow as he moves, as though he's worn out from a life spent in the saddle, facing down outlaws and Indians.

"What have we got, Bill?" asked Sheriff Leckie, climbing down from his horse.

"Looks like somebody fired a shotgun into Jim Bell's head," replied Mr. Osterman.

Shot! Mr. Moultray looked as shocked as I was.

"Who would do such a thing to a harmless old man?" he asked, dismounting.

"I'll tell you what," said Mr. Osterman. "I got a bad feeling I may have put Jim Bell in harm's way."

The sheriff looked up from where he and Mr. Moultray were tying their horses off to nearby trees. His eyes went narrow.

"Why would you say that?" the sheriff asked.

Mr. Osterman glanced over at Annie and me with the same look my father gets when he wants to say something to Mam that isn't for our ears. Sheriff Leckie looked at us, too.

"You the other Gillies kids?"

"Yes, sir," I said.

"You're the one who found the body?"

I'll admit I puffed up with pride to have the sheriff of Whatcom County ask me such a question.

"Yes, sir," I replied. "I am."

Sheriff Leckie turned to Mr. Osterman.

"Let's see what we got."

The remains of the cabin were smoldering now and the smoke stung my eyes as we stood in the clearing. Sheriff Leckie, Mr. Osterman, and Mr. Moultray rolled Mr. Bell's body over to get a look at his bashed-in head. They knelt there for a long time in the grass, talking amongst themselves. They made Annie and me keep our distance, so it was hard to make out what they were saying, but I caught bits and pieces.

"… crazy old fool wouldn't keep a gun to defend himself …"

"… too trusting … always taking in strays …"

It was curious the way they blamed Mr. Bell for getting himself murdered. Still, I knew what they were saying. Many a time when we were passing by Mr. Bell's cabin on the way to or from school, the old man would be waiting out on the trail to offer us children a sweet or a drink of water. But there were things about him—his yellow teeth and sour breath, the smell of his unwashed clothes, the way he laughed like he had some secret joke—that made me make excuses and get my brothers and sister away as fast as I could.

I listened some more.

"… got him in the back of the head …"

"… must have turned his back to go for something …"

"… or just caught unawares …"

Then, from Mr. Osterman, "You think the Indian

could have done this?"

An Indian! The thought of an Indian murdering a white settler was enough to send a tremor through every one of us standing in that clearing. If the Indians thought they could get away with killing one of us, they were just as liable to get the notion of starting an all-out war, aimed at driving every man, woman and child out of our homes.

When we crossed the prairie by wagon train six years ago, the old-timers told us hair-raising tales about how the savages were known to attack the trains and wipe out whole families—innocent people who wanted nothing more than to create new homes for themselves out of the wilderness. Settlers have only been in these parts for barely longer than I've been alive, and the Indians outnumber us by a long shot. Before we arrived, all they did was fish and hunt. That left a lot of land unspoken for, and in the past twenty years lumbermen and miners and homesteaders have been pleased to claim that land as their own. Wouldn't you know that the Indians would then turn around and complain that the territory belongs to them and we've got no business being here, even though they weren't using the land for anything much to speak of.

It's put into folks' heads from the cradle that if a white man lets an Indian get the upper hand, the next thing you know your scalp is as likely as not to be hanging off of his belt. We settlers are ever mindful of the fact that barely eight years ago Crazy Horse and his warriors massacred General Custer and his men at the Little Big Horn River, due east of us in Montana. The worry that even the friendly Indians might turn against us is enough to make every homesteader bolt the door at night and sleep with his rifle and an ax beside his bed, including my father. If an Indian killed Mr. Bell, none of us could sleep easy.

John and Will arrived back, winded from running the whole distance. "What's going on?" John asked, annoyed that he was missing out on something.

"They think an Indian might have done it," I told him.

"What Indian?"

"Just pay attention and maybe you'll find out."

He was irking me, making me miss out on important details. The blanket was back over Mr. Bell's body now, and the men were standing to continue their discussion, making it easier to hear them.

"I put out the word that I was looking for somebody to fix poles for me, and this morning Louie Sam shows up," Mr. Osterman was saying. "I could tell he was a bad type the minute I laid eyes on him, but I started walking the line with him down this way, pointing out what needed repairing. He was too slow-witted to catch on to what I was trying to get across to him. I'll tell you, he was hot-headed enough to send smoke signals through his ears when I told him I couldn't use him and sent him away."

"And this was just this morning?"

"That's correct, Sheriff. He came by the telegraph office early for a Sunday, maybe nine o'clock."

The sheriff checked his pocket watch.

"It's now a quarter past eleven."

"The timing's right. I left him on the trail not far from here a little more than an hour ago. I kept on going down the line. I figured Louie Sam headed back into town. But maybe he didn't. Maybe he found Jim Bell's place."

"I know Louie Sam." It was Bill Moultray talking now. "He's a Sumas, from the Canadian side. And I know his old man, too. They call him Mesatche Jack Sam."

"'Mean,'" said Sheriff Leckie, translating from Chinook, the trade jargon used by the various Indian bands in this area to make themselves understood to each other, and to us whites.

"You got it. Mean Jack's in jail up in New Westminster for murder."

This gave all three of them pause, until Mr. Osterman stated what we were all thinking: "The apple doesn't fall far from the tree."

If the father was a murdering Indian, so was the son likely to be. We had ourselves a suspect in the murder of Mr. James Bell, and his name was Louie Sam.

CHAPTER THREE

JOHN AND I AGREED THAT we should send Annie
home with Will, and that the two of us should stay at
Mr. Bell's place in case the sheriff had more questions
for us. But the men seemed to forget we were there.
They found long sticks and poked at the charred
remains of the cabin, which were still too hot to
touch. Mr. Osterman used the end of his stick to pick
up a blackened jug from what was left of Mr. Bell's
merchandise.

"My bet is Jim Bell caught that Indian helping
himself to his goods," he said.

"Hard to tell," replied Sheriff Leckie, flipping
through some tin cans that had exploded in the heat.
"Who's to say what's missing?"

"I found something!" called Mr. Moultray from the
kitchen end of the ruins.

We all turned to see Mr. Moultray using his thick
boots to kick a fire-warped metal box out of the ashes.
It sprang open, spilling a fortune in gold coins onto the
grass! The sheriff let a whistle out between his teeth.

"It don't look like no robbery to me," he said.

Mr. Osterman knelt down to count the coins, but the first one burned him when he tried to pick it up. "Goddamit!" he blasphemed, blowing on his fingers.

"There must be five hundred dollars there," said the sheriff.

"Louie Sam missed out on the big prize," remarked Mr. Moultray.

"But he might have taken Mr. Bell's horse," I said.

The men turned to me and John. They seemed surprised to find us still there. The sheriff rubbed his chin.

"Nobody's seen his horse this morning?" he asked.

"No, sir," I replied. "It was gone when we got here."

"If that Indian's on horseback, he could be ten miles away by now," said Mr. Moultray. "All the way to the border. Assuming he's heading for his tribe on the Canadian side."

"So he's a horse thief as well as a murderer," was all that Mr. Osterman had to add.

BUT JUST AFTER NOON, Robert Breckenridge, a neighbor from a couple of miles away, arrived leading a stray he said had turned up on his land and which he recognized as belonging to Mr. Bell. He had come by only meaning to return the horse, and was shocked by the sight of the cabin—shocked still further when the men told him what had befallen Mr. Bell. Mr.

Breckenridge related how just the day before he had seen a lone Indian lurking around near his spread, carrying a rifle, who claimed when challenged that he was hunting game. The men agreed that it stood to reason that the Indian Mr. Breckenridge saw could well have been Louie Sam, and that the rifle he was carrying was very likely the murder weapon.

Next thing you know Father arrived on Mae, our mare, telling John and me to go home. He'd heard enough from Will and Annie to make him come fetch us. I think he mostly came out of curiosity, though, because a minute later he was caught up in the mystery as Sheriff Leckie and Mr. Moultray told the whole story all over again. On hearing it a second time—with Mr. Breckenridge's additions—it was plain as day that Louie Sam was the culprit, even if he could no longer be called a horse thief. Murdering an innocent white man in cold blood was just like something a bad Indian would do.

At that point, Mr. Osterman gave a holler. He had been checking around Mr. Bell's property and had found tracks leading into the swamp. Sheriff Leckie told us all to stand back while he took a look, but even at a distance I could make out some faint dents in the grass that could easily have been made by moccasins. At the place where the footprints reached the swamp there were trampled rushes—as though a body had burst through them at a run.

"Louie Sam must have escaped this way," declared Mr. Osterman.

"Now hold on," said Sheriff Leckie. "A deer could have made this track as well as an Indian."

"But Sheriff," I blurted, "that renegade could be getting away!"

Father turned toward me, reminded of my presence.

"I thought I told you to go home."

"Don't be cross with the boy, Mr. Gillies," said Mr. Osterman. "George has been a real help today."

"So have I!" piped up John.

"Quiet, both of you," said Father, "or I'll send you on your way right now." Which John and I took to understand that we would be allowed to stay as long as we remembered our place.

Sheriff Leckie had been quietly thinking.

"That Indian has had a couple of hours to clear out of here. He'll be headed north. Once he's crossed the border, it's up to the Canadians what they do with him."

That made Mr. Breckenridge, a small man who makes up with spitfire what he lacks in height and breadth, hot under the collar.

"Jim Bell is one of us!" he said. "He's a Nooksack Valley man, and that Indian ought to pay for what he done in the Nooksack Valley!"

"I won't argue that with you, Bob," the sheriff replied, his words slow as molasses. "But we've got our laws and the Canadians have got theirs."

"If we start north now, we can catch him before he leaves the Territory," said Mr. Osterman. "If we let him get cross the border, there's no saying whether the Canadians will hand him over."

Mr. Breckenridge agreed. "You got to stop that savage before he gets away, Sheriff."

The sheriff pulled at his chin. "I suppose I best get started."

"I'll come with you," said Mr. Breckenridge. "You shouldn't face that red-skinned dog alone."

It was agreed that Mr. Breckenridge would go with Sheriff Leckie. The rest of us stayed behind to find out where the trail into the swamp led, with Mr. Osterman in the lead. It was hard going, trying to find bits of solid ground to set our boots upon. After five minutes my feet were wet and cold, but I wasn't about to complain about it for fear of looking like I couldn't keep up with the men. I glanced behind me to John to try to make out whether he was in the same discomfort as me. His pig-headed look told me that he was.

It was clever of that Indian to escape through the swamp, which swallowed up his footprints the same way it tried to swallow our boots. But Mr. Osterman did a good job of reading what signs as there were, finding a broken branch here, and a handkerchief stuck to a bramble there. We came across some cans of beans and bully beef that must have come from Mr. Bell's store, as though Louie Sam in his haste had dropped them. Strangest of all was an old pair of suspenders we found caught in some brambles. As we plunged onward, the men began to talk about what was on everyone's mind.

"Once the Nooksack hear about this, there's bound to be more trouble," said Mr. Moultray.

The Nooksack is the name of the local Indians on our side of the border, from which the river and our town took their names. On the Canadian side, it's the Sumas tribe. To hear the Indians tell it, they were all one big happy family until the International Border cut right through their hunting grounds twenty-five years ago, dividing them up. According to Mr. Breckenridge, who Father says considers himself to be an expert on just about everything, they still get together for wild heathen shindigs they call potlatches. Even though Louie Sam was a Sumas from the Canadian side, the worry was that he would go boasting to his cousins on the American side that he killed a white man. The Nooksack have been rumbling for years about this being their land. If they got the notion that getting rid of us settlers was as simple as shooting us like dogs, we could wind up with a full-scale uprising on our hands—just like what happened in Oregon and the Dakotas until the U.S. Army showed those Indians who was boss. The trouble was, the U.S. Army was nowhere in sight, the nearest outpost being three hundred miles south of us at Fort Walla Walla. The Indians of the Nooksack Valley knew we were pretty much defenseless, and that they had us outnumbered.

"We didn't have this kind of trouble when Bill Hampton was alive," Father remarked.

Mr. Hampton was the ferryman at The Crossing before he drowned and my friend Pete's father, Dave Harkness, took over. "Bill had a knack for talking to the Nooksack. They listened to him."

Mr. Osterman let out a hard laugh, obviously not sharing Father's good opinion of Mr. Hampton.

"That's because he was shacked up with one of their women and had himself a couple of Indian kids." He was talking about Agnes, Mr. Hampton's Indian wife, who lives near us on Sumas Creek with her two half-breed sons. He added, "We got to make an example of Louie Sam before the Nooksack go getting ideas."

"No question about that," Father agreed.

"Let's see what the sheriff has to say when he gets back," Mr. Moultray told them.

He was a natural leader, Mr. Moultray—cool and always thinking. He was the one leading the talk in our corner of the Washington Territory about pressing the Union to make us a full state with our own laws, and not just a territory ruled by the president from Washington, D.C.

We reached a big old log that was sticking up out of the swamp at an angle and climbed up on it. On the other side of it, we could see sunken footprints where Louie Sam had made a long jump off the log into the bog. From there the bush got thicker and the trail petered out. The men decided that there was no point continuing. If Louie Sam was going to be caught, it was up to the sheriff to do it.

WE RETURNED TO MR. BELL's burned-out cabin. The ruins were cooler now. It was easier to pick through the remains, but there was nothing much left. It seemed Mr. Bell didn't own much to speak of, even before the fire turned it all to ash. Nothing but the five hundred dollars in gold he had in that strong box.

"I'll keep it in the safe at my store until it's decided what's to be done with it," volunteered Mr. Moultray.

"What about the body?" asked Father.

"May as well bring him back to my place," said Mr. Moultray. "He'll keep in my shed until he's buried. His horse can stay in my stable until somebody decides who gets him."

Father remarked, "I suppose somebody needs to tell Mrs. Bell what happened."

The men all fell silent at that. Nobody was stepping up to volunteer for that particular detail. The situation was complicated, what with Mrs. Bell having up and left Mr. Bell a year ago to go live with Pete's pa.

Father remembered something about Mr. Osterman.

"Your wife Maggie is Dave Harkness's sister, isn't she?"

"That she is," he replied.

Mr. Moultray saw what Father was driving at and finished his thought.

"That's practically family," he said to Mr. Osterman. "It's only fitting that you should be the one to tell Mrs. Bell." He added by way of lessening the weight of the duty, "I don't reckon she'll be too sorrowful."

There was another long silence. From the way Father glanced at John and me, I got the feeling that more would have been said on the matter if we boys had not been present.

CHAPTER FOUR

IT TURNED OUT THAT SHERIFF LECKIE and Robert
Breckenridge didn't make it to Canada on Sunday
afternoon. They got stopped by the discovery of a new
witness—who turned out to be none other than Pete
Harkness. Outside the schoolhouse at lunchtime on
Monday, I got the full story from Pete.

"I was coming back from Lynden—"

"What were you doing way over there?" I asked
him. Lynden is a good five miles west of Nooksack.

"I was running an errand for my pa. Stop
interrupting!"

Pete likes to hear himself talk. He may not be the
smartest boy in school, but I know from my little
sister Annie that all the girls in the classroom—from
the first grade on up—think he's handsome with
his blue eyes and wavy hair. He's tall and broad-
shouldered, and has a way of believing that his good
looks mean he's always right.

"So I was heading along the road from Lynden
back home to The Crossing," he continued, "when I

saw Louie Sam coming toward me, walking in the other direction. Let me tell you, the look on that Indian's face struck me with terror—so dark was it and filled with evil. There was murder in his eyes."

"Did you see the rifle that he used to kill Mr. Bell?"

"Damn right, I did! Of course, I didn't know at the time that he used it to murder Mr. Bell."

Tom Breckenridge came over and joined us.

"Pete saw Louie Sam yesterday," I told him, "walking along the Lynden road."

"If I'd seen him," Tom replied, "he wouldn't be walking no more."

He spit in the dirt. Tom is Pete's age, but small and wiry like his father. And—like his father—Tom is full of tough talk trying to make up for his size. Ignoring his bluster, I turned my attention back to Pete.

"So what happened next?"

"When I got to The Crossing, Uncle Bill was there, telling Pa that Mr. Bell was dead," Pete said.

"How did Mrs. Bell take the news?" I asked.

"Why should I care?" proclaimed Pete.

I should have known better than to ask. Pete has no fondness for his more-or-less stepmother, Mrs. Bell, nor for her son Jimmy, who's living under Pete's roof now like they're supposed to be brothers.

"Anyway," he went on, "when I told Pa about seeing the evil look on that redskin, he said that I had to tell Sheriff Leckie what I saw right away. He even let me saddle up Star. I headed for the sheriff's office in Nooksack at a gallop, and got there just in time— because the sheriff and your pa," he said, nodding to Tom, "were just about to set off north in search of Louie Sam."

"And the whole time, Louie Sam was heading west, on the Lynden road!"

"Exactly. If it hadn't been for me coming across him like that, they would have headed off on a wild goose chase to end all. As it was, Louie Sam managed to hide himself among a bunch of Nooksack in a camp they got near Lynden."

"So his *tillicums* took him in," I remarked.

That's more Chinook lingo: *tillicum* means friend.

"Sheriff Leckie tried to talk their chief into handing him over, but the chief said they hadn't seen him."

"Lying Indians!" declared Tom.

"Is there another kind?" replied Pete. "The sheriff said the chief had twenty or more braves with him, so there was nothing he could do but wait and hope that Louie Sam might make a break for it. Finally, he reckoned there was no point in waiting any longer. That Indian could have slipped away into the forest any time he wanted."

"Heading for his people north of the border," I ventured to guess.

"That's what the sheriff thinks," said Pete. "He

and Tom's pa headed up the trail for Canada this morning."

"Tell me something I don't know," said Tom.

PETE'S ACCOUNT OF SEEING Louie Sam clinched it. If anybody had had doubts about that Indian's guilt before, it was impossible to deny it now. The way everybody had it figured, Louie Sam must have come across Mr. Bell's cabin shortly after his falling out with Mr. Osterman and decided to help himself to the supplies within. Given the temper on that Indian, it's no stretch to imagine that the slightest complaint on the matter from Mr. Bell would have sent him on the rampage. So he waited until Mr. Bell's back was turned and he let him have it. But, on the other hand, people said Mr. Bell would share a meal with anybody passing by, so why would he have denied a few cans of beans to an Indian who was holding a rifle? Why would he have risked his life for that? I voiced all of this to Pete.

"You think too much," was his reply. "Louie Sam killed Mr. Bell. That's all you got to know."

"How's Jimmy?" I asked.

"How should I know?" Pete snapped.

"It's his pa that's dead," I said.

Jimmy Bell is my brother John's age and I don't know him well, but I couldn't help but feel sorry for him—especially since it mustn't be easy for him, with his mother taking him away from his father to go live with the Harknesses.

"Jimmy hated his pa," replied Pete.

"Why?"

"Why do you ask so many stupid questions, George Gillies?"

With that, Pete went off to join a ball game a few of the boys had started up in the field behind the school. My brother John was one of those boys, and so was Jimmy Bell. Jimmy was a quiet type, plump and big for his age—not really one to stand out at sports or in school. I watched him take his turn stepping up to bat, swinging, missing an easy ball—cursing. If he was sad about his pa it didn't show. So maybe Pete was right. Maybe he *did* hate his father—or at least had no warm feelings for him. But then I thought, maybe Jimmy was feeling more angry than sad about what happened. I guessed that I might feel that way, too, if it was my father who had been murdered in cold blood.

MR. BRECKENRIDGE CAME BACK from Canada that very afternoon. We heard this news from our neighbor, Mr. Pratt, who came to our mill late in the day. He heard it from Mr. Hopkins who works at the new hotel in town—who had been at The Crossing when Mr. Breckenridge arrived at Bill Moultray's store with the tale of his journey. News travels up and down the valley so fast, it's almost like the telegraph line.

"The sheriff and Bob Breckenridge went to see the Canadian justice of the peace in Sumas, a Mr. Campbell," said Mr. Pratt, who's a natural storyteller and plays the fiddle when there's a dance in town. Like Father, he's a Scot by birth. "The justice listened to all the evidence Sheriff Leckie presented and agreed that Louie Sam was the likely culprit. It turns out that Justice Campbell's the one who put Louie Sam's old man in jail for murder, so it came as no surprise to him that the son had followed in his father's footsteps."

"What's he planning to do about it?" asked Father as he poured a sack of Mr. Pratt's wheat into the hopper, getting ready to grind it.

"He issued a warrant for Louie Sam's arrest. But, the way Bob tells it, the sheriff didn't altogether trust this Campbell fellow. The Canadians have different ways, different laws. So the sheriff talked Campbell into letting him ride with him to take Louie Sam into custody, to make sure justice is served. Bob and the sheriff parted ways at that point, and Bob came back here to spread the word."

"And this Justice Campbell expects the Sumas to hand Louie Sam over just like that? Because he has a warrant?" Father's eyebrow was cocked, meaning he thought this was a daft notion.

"Aye, that's the question, Peter," replied Mr. Pratt,

with his own knowing look. "That's the question."

Before leaving, Mr. Pratt also told us that plans had been made for Mr. Bell's funeral. Those who were interested in paying their respects were to meet at the Hausers' cabin on Wednesday. Judging by the mood in the valley, Mr. Pratt expected to see every man in the district there, ready to show the local Indians by force of numbers that they would not let the murder of a white man go unnoticed, or unpunished.

CHAPTER FIVE

ON WEDNESDAY MORNING, the day of Mr. Bell's funeral, my mother and father were arguing. There were no raised voices—that isn't Mam's way. But when she is displeased, you know it. I could tell just by looking at her when Father and I came in from milking that something was eating at her. Mam was short-tempered as she tried dishing up breakfast, hampered by the big roundness of her middle—that out of delicacy we boys were not supposed to mention.

Finally, Father told Mam to sit down and let Annie do the serving. In that, she obeyed him. But her mouth was still tight as a drum as she helped Isabel with her porridge.

"Anna, it's the man's funeral," Father said out of the blue, as though picking up on a discussion he and Mam had been having earlier.

"I have no argument with you going to show Mr. Bell his due. It's this foolish talk I can't abide."

I was curious about what talk she was referring to.

"You do not appreciate the seriousness of the

matter," replied Father, using his serious voice to prove the point.

"I get along just fine with the Indians," Mam said.

"When do you ever have business with the Indians?"

"Agnes Hampton often brings me berries in exchange for a few eggs. Or one of her boys will bring me a hare, or a brace of quail."

"That squaw was never Mrs. Hampton," Father replied.

From the way he said it, there was a meaning behind the words that he did not intend for us children to grasp. But being more experienced in the world than my brothers and sisters, I knew what he was getting at—that the Hamptons had never been properly married. Mam was silenced for a moment by that remark, though not for long.

"It seems some folks are more easily forgiven on that account than others."

Now she was talking about Pete's father and Mrs. Bell, who also lived as man and wife without the benefit of a preacher.

Father came back with, "There's sinning, and then there's sinning."

I wasn't at all sure what Father meant by that, but Mam seemed to understand him just fine.

"It's not those boys' fault they were born half-breeds," she said. "And just because there's one bad

Indian, that doesn't mean you men have cause to tar all the rest of them with the same brush."

At that, Father put his foot down.

"I'll thank you to leave men's business to the men. This conversation is hereby over."

Mam's mouth was tighter than ever.

I CAUGHT UP WITH FATHER as he was heading from our cabin down to the mill, our dog Gypsy following us and barking into the woods surrounding the path. Something had her excited. I hoped it wasn't a bear or a cougar.

"Father?"

"What is it, George?"

"I thought you liked Mr. Hampton."

"I liked him just fine."

"Then why do you think he was a sinner? I mean, a worse sinner than Mr. Harkness?"

Father rubbed his chin with the flat of his hand.

"George," he said, "you're almost a man now. You need to understand the way things work. God in his wisdom created different types of people. That's the way he wanted it. So when those different types of people …" He stopped himself, then started again. "When it comes to marrying and raising bairns, those types are meant to stick to their own kind. Are you following me?"

I was not, in fact, following him too well. But I was

a man, or almost a man. Father had just said so. And a man has to understand these things.

"Sure I do," I said.

"Good. Now get yourself to school and put some learning in that head of yours."

The settlers built the one-room schoolhouse on the western edge of Nooksack a few years ago. It takes a good hour of walking for John, Will, Annie, and me to get there, following the trail that leads into town—the one that passes by Mr. Bell's cabin. Even three days later there's a bitter smell in the air from the fire as we go by. Every morning since it happened, John and Will had wanted to linger at the Bell place and explore. I had to bark at them to hurry along, lest we were late for school and Miss Carmichael, the schoolma'am, kept us in at recess as punishment.

Jimmy Bell wasn't at school Wednesday morning. Neither was Pete Harkness. Miss Carmichael had to yell at us kids to pay attention. Nobody had a mind for grammar or sums. All anybody wanted to talk about was the funeral, and whether Jimmy and Pete would be there. And whether Mrs. Bell would show up. I've seen Annette Bell in town, and a few times when I was over at The Crossing to visit Pete. She is young— younger than Mam—and she comes from Australia, which makes her a curiosity. Folks around here come from Great Britain and Canada and various states, but she's the only one from Australia. Everybody knows that they send convicts to Australia.

It's hard to picture Mrs. Bell being in love with old Mr. Bell. Pete's father, on the other hand, is tall and strong and broad-shouldered from pulling the cable ferry that spans the Nooksack River—the sort of man that some women, Mam is willing to grant, find handsome. It seems the Harkness men are lucky that way.

Miss Carmichael told the senior class to take out our slates and do the algebra she'd written on the blackboard. Over the squeaking of chalk, I heard Abigail Stevens whisper to Kitty Pratt, "Mrs. Bell only married Mr. Bell for his money."

Abigail is sixteen and—I supposed—knows about such things. I remembered the five hundred dollars in gold coin that Sheriff Leckie found in Mr. Bell's cabin, and thought that maybe she was right.

At noon, Miss Carmichael—who suffers from nervous headaches—told us not to come back to school after the dinner break. I started on my way home with John, Will, and Annie, but it wasn't long before a different destination came to mind. The funeral was due to get started at one o'clock. All the men of the Nooksack Valley would be there, and I intended to be there, too. I told John to walk on home with the younger kids. But being stubborn by nature,

John was not about to be left behind. So Will wound up walking Annie home, while John and I headed over to the Hauser place.

"Why is the funeral happening at the Hausers'?" I pondered as we walked. "Why not at church?"

Nooksack has two churches to choose from, the Presbyterian and the Methodist. We Gillies are Presbyterians, being Scots.

"Don't you know that old man Bell was godless?" replied John.

"Is that what Jimmy told you?"

"Jimmy says he was a downright heathen. Worse than an Indian, because he should know better."

"Is that why Jimmy and his mam left him?"

"I don't know why they left," said John.

"It's like there were two different Mr. Bells," I mused. "Some folks say he was a nice old man, generous to a fault. Others say he was strange in the head. It's sad his own son doesn't care that he's dead."

John had no comment on that.

THE HAUSERS' FARM IS on the opposite side of Nooksack from our place—south of town instead of north. It's just a stone's throw from The Crossing, where Bill Moultray has his store and Dave Harkness has his ferry. When John and I got there, the long track leading up to the cabin was clogged with wagons. Dozens of horses were tethered to bushes and to the split-rail fence surrounding a small corral. Still more were inside the corral, poking their noses through the fence to snatch mouthfuls of clover. I recognized Star, the Harknesses' gelding. Up closer to the cabin, John and I came across Mae, tied by her reins to a cedar sapling. When John spoke her name, she raised her head and gave us a funny look, like she was wondering what in heck we were doing there. Then she went back to cropping grass.

Several men were standing outside on the veranda, smoking and talking quietly. Among them were Bill Osterman, the telegraph man who'd led our search through the swamp, and Tom Breckenridge's father, who had gone up north with Sheriff Leckie. Dave Harkness was with them, too. Mr. Osterman's face was grim.

"Are we going to allow the Canadians to interfere in our business?" he was saying. "Does a murdering Indian deserve a trial, same as a civilized man?"

"He most certainly does not!" declared Mr. Breckenridge.

Bert Hopkins, a shorty in specs who runs the new Nooksack Hotel, spoke up.

"What can we do about it? The Canadians have got him in custody by now."

"We got a jail right here in town that would hold him just fine," said Mr. Harkness.

"That's what I'm thinking," agreed Mr. Osterman.

At that moment, my friend Pete came outside.

"Pa, Uncle Bill," he said, Mr. Osterman being married to his auntie, "they're ready to start."

The men exchanged more grim looks, and filed into the cabin.

"Pete!" I called.

He turned, frowning at the sight of John and me as we reached the veranda.

"This is no place for kids," he said.

That made my blood boil. Sometimes Pete acts like such a big bug, just because he's got a year's head start on me.

"We're the ones who found the body," John shot back. "We got a right to be here."

"There's serious talk going on inside," Pete told us.

"If you can hear it, I can hear it," I said.

"And me," John was quick to add.

"I'm not wasting my time arguing with you two," Pete replied, and went into the cabin.

John and I went right in after him.

THE CABIN WAS SO PACKED with men that it was easy for John and me not to be noticed by Father, who was on the other side of the room. Mrs. Bell was not there, but her son Jimmy was. A wooden box containing Mr. Bell was propped up on chairs at one end of the room. Jimmy stood near the casket, wearing a sullen expression, like he didn't want to be there. John and

I listened while several of the men said nice things about Mr. Bell. Bill Moultray gave a speech first, then Mr. Breckenridge spoke, and Mr. Hauser, but neither Jimmy nor Mr. Harkness had anything to say about the dead man.

When Mr. Osterman got up to speak, he took a different tone. He didn't talk about what a good man Mr. Bell was. He talked about what an outrage it was the way Mr. Bell died. He talked about how, in the absence of the U.S. Army, it fell to the men of the Nooksack Valley to protect their wives and children from what had happened to Mr. Bell. An example had to be made, he said.

"This is the new frontier. Like the great frontiersmen before us, we must defend what's ours. It's up to us to see that civilized justice is done."

"Hear, hear!" shouted Mr. Harkness.

The room suddenly got loud, with everybody nodding his head and agreeing with his neighbor that what Mr. Osterman said was dead to right. The Indians had to know who was in charge. A proposal was made by Mr. Osterman that the men present should form the Nooksack Vigilance Committee— just as other frontier towns had done to uphold law and order. Mr. Harkness declared that the first order of business of the Nooksack Vigilance Committee was to make sure that Louie Sam paid for what he did to Mr. Bell. A plan took shape to set out that very day north to Canada to make sure justice was served against the renegade Indian—for nobody present was in a mood for assuming the Canadians would do what was right, what was needed.

For the first time, Father spoke up.

"According to Mr. Breckenridge," he said, "Sheriff Leckie and the Canadian justice of the peace have gone to Sumas to make the arrest. We should wait until the sheriff comes back. See what he has to say about the situation."

"Maybe that's how things are done where you come from, Mr. Gillies," replied Mr. Osterman, "but we need surer justice!"

"And swifter!" It was Dave Harkness talking now. Pete was at his elbow, puffed up— trying to look like as big a man as his pa. "Why wait? That Indian needs his neck stretched."

"Hold on a minute," said Mr. Stevens, Abigail's father. "They got procedures across the border. We could find ourselves in an international incident if we act out of turn."

"It was one of us that was killed," called out Mr. Harkness. "It should be us that settles it!"

Everybody was talking and shouting at once now, smelling blood.

"But what if he's holed up with the Sumas?" said Mr. Hopkins. "There's hundreds of them. You think they're going to just let us waltz in and take one of their own away?"

"Then we'll show them we got the numbers to stand up to them!" shouted Mr. Harkness.

"We should dress up like warriors!" Mr. Breckenridge called out. "Give those savages a taste of their own medicine!"

There was mayhem now, everybody talking so loud as to wake up even poor Mr. Bell. Mr. Osterman got up on Mrs. Hauser's table and held up his hands to quiet them down.

"Spread the word to those who aren't here. We meet at The Crossing at nightfall."

"Wait!" It was Father speaking. Suddenly, all eyes were on him. "I'd like to hear what Mr. Moultray has to say about this expedition."

Everyone turned to Bill Moultray, the richest man among them and the one who holds the most weight. His brow was furrowed, like he was giving serious consideration to what was being proposed.

"Well, Bill?" said Mr. Osterman. "What do you say?"

You could hear a pin drop as the men waited for his blessing.

"I say," he pronounced at last, "that this is the time for every man to stand up and do what's right."

And so it was agreed. The Nooksack Vigilance Committee would set out that night in disguise and under the cover of darkness to find Louie Sam, and avenge the death of James Bell.

CHAPTER SIX

AFTER THE SPEECHES, WE GATHERED in a clearing on the Hausers' land where the Hausers had buried two of their babies that died. John and I watched from the trees as they put Mr. Bell's casket in the ground and filled in the hole, marking the spot with a small wooden cross to match those on the babies' graves. Heathen or not, Mr. Bell was buried as a Christian. Soon as that was done, the men found their horses and wagons and set off for home to ready themselves for the night's adventure. There was discussion about what form their warrior costumes should take. Somebody suggested they should paint their faces to make themselves look frightening, the way the Nooksack Indians and their cousins the Sumas do at their potlatches.

Father spotted John and me as he walked to fetch Mae. He was not pleased to see us.

"Why aren't you two in school?"

"Miss Carmichael dismissed us," I said. Then I couldn't stop myself from asking, "Are you going with them tonight?"

"Never you mind what I'm doing, George."

"But Mr. Osterman said every man is needed."

Father reddened. He was angry now.

"You two were inside there?"

It was John who answered with his usual cheek, "Yes, sir. It's our duty to defend the Nooksack Valley."

Father took a measure of John, like he was about to get angrier still. But, instead, he cooled right down.

"I appreciate that, John," Father said. "The best thing you can do to help is to keep watch over your mam and the wee ones."

I don't know what made me say it—maybe it was the way that Father was looking at John like he was just as much of a man as I was—but without thinking about it I announced, "I'm going with you!"

Father looked at me and let out a laugh.

"To raid an Indian village? Nae, laddie, you are staying put." With that he climbed up on Mae and started her away at a trot, calling back to us, "You boys get yourselves home."

John started hoofing it down the track, following Father and Mae. I stayed put.

"Well, c'mon," he said, turning back. "What are you waiting for?"

"Go on ahead," I told him. "I've got some business to attend to."

"The only business you got is minding Father."

"Go on," I said. "I'll be there soon."

"Fine with me, if what you want is a whipping."

With a shrug, John walked on. In truth I had no business whatsoever to keep me there. My gaze fell upon Pete, who looked as irritated as I felt. I walked over to him.

"What do you want?" he said.

"Nothing!" I barked back, matching his tone. "Can't a fella say hello?"

"I'm not in a 'hello-ing' mood right now."

Pete started walking down the path. I fell in beside him.

"Aren't you waiting for your pa?" I asked him.

"He went ahead."

"He left you behind?"

"Yes, he left me behind. What about it?"

"He left you behind with us kids?"

Pete stopped, turned. "You want a fat lip, George?"

He held his fist up, curled tight. He would have hit me, too. Pete's the type to act first and think about it later. But I decided to take a higher road.

"I'm going with them tonight," I said.

I could see that took the wind out of Pete's sails.

"Your pa said you could?"

"Doesn't matter what he says. I'm going. It's our duty to defend the Nooksack Valley," I added, borrowing the phrase that had served John so well with Father.

Pete got a snide look.

"And how do you plan to do that without a horse?"

He raised a good point. Father would be riding Mae. Our mule, Ulysses, was only good for pulling the plough and sometimes the buckboard wagon. But then an idea struck me.

"I know where there's a horse."

"Where?"

"They put Mr. Bell's horse in Mr. Moultray's livery. I don't reckon Mr. Bell would complain about me borrowing him, considering the purpose."

Pete's wheels were turning.

"I'm going with you," he said.

"You're not invited." Now that I had the upper hand, I wasn't about to let it go.

Pete came back with, "You're taking me with you, or I'm telling your pa and Mr. Moultray what you're up to."

He had me. There was nothing I could do but give in. Besides, the truth was that I wouldn't mind his company. It was a dangerous road we were about to travel.

I WENT HOME AND DID my chores. At supper, Annie told Mam I was coming down with something, all because when I was splitting wood and she was feeding the chickens she kept prattling on asking me what names I liked for the new baby, and I told her in no uncertain terms that I did not feel like talking. Mam held her hand to my forehead and agreed that I felt warm. She told me she wanted me to go to bed right after I was finished eating. Little did she know that she was aiding my plan to join the men at The Crossing, because I knew I could easily slip out the window from the back room we kids shared. I was careful not to look at John while we sat at the table, for fear he would see in my eyes what was on my mind.

All this time, Father was busy gathering his disguise. When at last he appeared, I thought Mam's jaw would hit the floor.

"What on earth!" she cried.

Over his head was a gunnysack from the mill, with holes cut in it for his eyes. Mam's petticoat was hanging from around his neck. The layers of cloth flounced over his shoulders when he walked, something like feathers on a fluffy bird. Annie laughed, thinking she'd never seen such a funny sight as our Father at that moment. But Isabel was frightened and would not stop crying until Father removed the gunnysack from his head. Once she got over her shock, Mam was furious that he'd ruined her petticoat by cutting holes in it for his arms. She barely said good-bye to him as he headed out to saddle Mae. It seemed like the argument they were having that morning was still going on.

I excused myself from the table, making like I was too ill to finish my stew. In the back room, I quickly put on my jacket and my boots. That's when John came in. If he was surprised to see me getting ready to escape, he didn't show it.

"So you're doing this, then," he said.

"You keep your mouth shut about it, you hear me, John Gillies?"

"I hear you." He kept his voice low, mindful lest Mam hear us from the front room. He added, "You better tell me all about it when you get back."

I RAN MOST OF THE WAY to The Crossing. Dusk was settling in, making it hard to find my footing on the trail, but I kept moving fast. I had no fear of being found out by Father, who was well ahead of me on Mae. But if I was late, I knew Pete would take Mr. Bell's horse and leave without me.

The Crossing is almost a village unto itself. Mr. Moultray built his store near to the ferry crossing, and farmers come from miles around to sell their goods and buy supplies. He's got his livery stable next door, in which he boards wagon and stagecoach teams journeying along the Whatcom Trail. He boards passengers in the rooms above his store. Between the farmers and the travelers, Father says he must do fine business.

By the time I reached the large clearing outside

the livery stable, there must have been close to a hundred men and horses gathered there. It was fully dark now. Many of the men carried lanterns; all of them had rifles by their sides. They were a strange and frightening sight, dressed in sundry getups, many of them wearing skirts and petticoats—like Father's—borrowed from their wives. Others wore their coats inside out, so that the fur linings made them look like hairy beasts. Many had their faces painted, like Indians on the warpath—darkened with charcoal, with a flash of red across their eyes. I picked out my father seated on Mae, his face darkened with smudge since I last saw him, and our hunting rifle resting in the crook of his arm.

I skirted around them, keeping to the shadows. I found Pete inside Mr. Moultray's barn. He had Mr. Bell's horse saddled with borrowed tack.

"You took your sweet time getting here," Pete said.

"It's easy for you, living next door," I pointed out.

All Pete had to do was walk a hundred yards from the ferryman's house and he was at Mr. Moultray's store and livery.

We waited inside the livery for the Nooksack Vigilance Committee to depart. Pete and I opened the livery stable door just enough so we could listen, and watch. Mr. Moultray, as the natural leader, spoke to them before they set off.

"We came here from far away, from many states

and many countries," he said. "All we found when we got here was a trail left by the gold diggers twenty years ago, and the stumps left behind by the lumber barons. We cleared this land with our bare hands. We planted crops and raised cattle. We put the telegraph through. We built churches and a school. We built a town." Here he paused, the way my father pauses when he's reading the Bible out loud to us to let the important bits sink in. "We can't let the Indians threaten everything we've created here. We can't give them the notion that we lack the will to defend what's ours. Louie Sam took a life. He took one of our own. The dictates of civilization tell us that there is only one way that amends can be made."

"Hang him!" someone shouted.

A loud cry of approval went up from the men. The punishment for murder was hanging. Everybody knew that. Yet when I looked over to Father, I could see by the light of the lantern he was holding that he was not among those who were cheering. His face was serious and stern, made more so by the blackening he'd smeared over it. I couldn't understand him. Why was he not cheering with the rest of them, when the need to take action was so clear?

"Let's go!" called out Dave Harkness.

He spurred Star and rode up beside his brother-in-law, Mr. Osterman. The two of them set off in the lead, along with Mr. Moultray. Mr. Breckenridge and

Mr. Hopkins followed them. The rest of the men and horses fell in behind. There were so many that it took several minutes for them to form a parade, following the acknowledged leaders up the Whatcom Trail to Canada in clumps of twos and threes. My father rode alone, toward the rear.

As soon as the last man was out of sight, Pete led Mr. Bell's horse out of the stable. "What do we do for light?" I asked. It was a clear night, but lit by only a sliver of moon rising over the trees.

"We do without," Pete said. "You want them to look back and spot us?"

I supposed he was right, but the idea of riding through the woods in the pitch black made me nervous. There were wild cats and wolves about who would just love a taste of horsemeat. In the time I hesitated, Pete climbed up on Mr. Bell's horse in the front position and took up the reins.

"Hold on," I said. "This was my idea. I should ride up front."

"Quit arguing and get on board," Pete replied.

There was nothing for me to do but climb up into the saddle behind Pete. Mr. Bell's gelding was a sturdy sixteen hander, well able to hold our weight. Pete gave him a kick and he started off after the other horses, like he didn't need to be told where to go.

All he needed to do was follow the pack.

CHAPTER SEVEN

THE MEN WERE QUIET AS THEY RODE from The
Crossing, following the Whatcom Trail as it became
Nooksack Avenue, the main street of the town, then
continuing north and east to the outskirts of the
homesteaders' farms and beyond. By then we were
surrounded by untamed forest. All I could hear ahead
of us was the soft thud of hooves on the trail and the
odd twig snapping. After a while, the stars came out
and the wilderness seemed less black. Still, we made
slow progress, for not even the most eager of the men
was willing to risk breaking his horse's leg by pushing
him past a quick walk in the dark. I dared not say a
word to Pete even in a whisper, knowing how my voice
would carry. We rode this way for well over an hour,
until suddenly we heard talking ahead.

Pete and I jumped down from the horse and led
it by the reins up closer to the posse. We saw in a
clearing ahead that many of the men had dismounted.
Their lanterns formed a ring of light as they gathered
around someone or something. I signaled for Pete to

stay put with the horse, and I crept ahead through the trees so I could hear what was going on without being detected. I recognized Sheriff Leckie's voice coming from the middle of the circle of men and I realized our posse must have met up with him on the trail on his way back from Canada. He was telling the others what had happened since Mr. Breckenridge left him and the Canadian justice of the peace, William Campbell, two days earlier.

"I'll tell you one thing," the sheriff was saying, "they got a different way of handling the Indian problem up there. Got them all convinced that the bloody Queen of England is their Great Mother."

Sheriff Leckie relayed how he had gone with Justice Campbell to the Sumas Indian village, where Louie Sam came from. According to the sheriff, Justice Campbell entered into considerable discussions with the Sumas chiefs—more discussion than was necessary, in the sheriff's opinion. At last they agreed to hand the renegade over. When they laid eyes on Louie Sam, he appeared not even a little bit remorseful for what he did to Mr. Bell. The sheriff recounted how Justice Campbell explained to him in simple English that he was accused of murder, just like his father, Mesatche Jack Sam, had been before him. He explained there would be a trial with witnesses, just like his old man had, but that in the meantime Louie Sam would have to come with him to jail. Sheriff Leckie said that Louie Sam was peaceable enough, not kicking up a fuss when Justice Campbell put the handcuffs on him.

Dave Harkness said, "You mean to say you left that Indian there, warming himself inside a Canadian jail?"

"If letting a heathen murderer sit in jail with three squares a day is the Canadian idea of justice served, then we got a problem," stated Mr. Osterman.

There was a good deal of agreement among the men. Then my father spoke up, raising his voice above the others so that he would be sure to be heard.

"Justice Campbell promised there would be a trial," he said. "*That's* justice served."

A hush fell over the men. Nobody was rushing to agree with Father, the way they had with Mr. Osterman.

"If I'm hearing you right, Mr. Gillies," replied Mr. Osterman, "you recommend that the Indian deserves some kind of leniency."

"Give 'em an inch, they'll take a yard!" spat Mr. Harkness.

The other men took up the call for action. But Father wouldn't quit talking. In fact, the more they shouted him down, the more he seemed determined to have his say.

"We set out to make sure Louie Sam paid for what he did according to the law," Father shouted above them. "We should let him stand trial."

It's just like my father to speak his mind like that. Sometimes I think he goes out of his way to hold an opinion that's contrary to what most people hold to be true. What made him think he was right and everybody else was wrong? Why couldn't he just go along? For the first time in my life, I was embarrassed for him—embarrassed *by* him.

"Would you have us leave the job half done?" asked Mr. Breckenridge. "Maybe that's how you do things in the Old Country, Mr. Gillies, but it isn't how we do things around here."

"Louie Sam can not be allowed to spread lies in a court of law," declared Mr. Osterman. "Are we agreed?"

There was loud accord. I could see Father looking around as though expecting to find at least one man in the posse who wasn't set against him. But it seemed there was none. Father said no more.

Sheriff Leckie spoke: "I want to be clear. I have no authority on the Canadian side, nor can I allow you men to act on my authority. But this much I can tell you. Justice Campbell left the Indian in the hands of two constables, Jim Steele and Thomas York."

"Thomas York," said Mr. Moultray. "I've had dealings with him. He's a wily old Scot."

Someone called out, "One of your countrymen, is he not, Mr. Gillies?"

"Let's hope he's not as soft-hearted as you!" shouted someone else.

"Or soft-headed!" came another jibe from the crowd.

There was great laughter at that, from everyone but my father.

"How comes Thomas York to be a constable?" asked Mr. Moultray.

"He was deputized this afternoon for the purpose, by his son-in-law—Justice Campbell—along with the other fella, Steele. They're to bring the accused to the town of New Westminster in the morning, to the nearest courthouse."

I noticed a look passing between Mr. Harkness and Mr. Osterman.

"Over our dead bodies," said Dave Harkness.

Mr. Osterman asked, "Where might Louie Sam be now?"

"He's being held in Mr. York's farmhouse for the night."

"Where would we find this farmhouse?" Mr. Harkness asked.

"At Sumas Prairie, no more than six miles from here."

SHERIFF LECKIE RODE ON back to Nooksack shortly thereafter, leaving the leaders of the posse to chew over the news he'd brought them. Our prospects had changed considerably. No longer were the men facing the frightening possibility of fighting the Sumas

Indians in order to seize Louie Sam. Now their task was much simpler, there being only two constables at a farmhouse to be dealt with, one of them an old man. The mood lightened among the men, some of them joking that the Indian would soon be guest of honour at his own necktie party. But Mr. Hopkins pointed out that while Mr. York was old and feeble, they knew nothing about the second constable, Steele. And both men would be armed.

"There's a hundred of us against two of them," shouted Mr. Harkness. "Let them try and stop us!"

That started another round of cheering. Mr. Moultray, who hadn't said much up until now, quieted everybody down.

"Our purpose is to take Louie Sam," he declared in his speech-giving voice. "I will not be party to spilling the blood of Thomas York, nor of the other constable. Let no other white man be harmed in this sorry business."

At that, the posse calmed down. The five leaders— Mr. Moultray, Mr. Osterman, Mr. Harkness, Mr. Hopkins, and Mr. Breckenridge—went off to confer by themselves for a little while, and when they returned to the group they announced they had a plan. They proposed that one of our number be sent ahead to the York farm as a scout. Dave Harkness put forward his friend Jack Simpson, a coach driver for Mr. Moultray's livery stable, as the best candidate for the job, since Jack is an amiable sort and might do well at winning Mr. York's trust. Also, Jack was easily made to look like an ordinary traveler, having not blackened his face like many of the men had done, and changing his costume was only a matter of taking his inside-out coat and putting it to rights. Jack was dispatched with instructions to tell Mr. York he was in need of a bed for the night, and to that way gain entrance to the farmhouse. The posse would follow within two hours.

That left the rest of the men to cool their heels and rest their horses. Some lit campfires. Others took the chance to claim a few winks of sleep. I was about to go back to Pete and fill him in on all I'd heard when, wouldn't you know it, a whinny comes from out of the darkness, and there's Pete—riding up on Mr. Bell's horse. The men were instantly on alert for trouble.

"Who goes there?" shouted Dave Harkness.

He took aim with his rifle in the general direction of Pete, his finger twitching over the trigger.

CHAPTER EIGHT

"DON'T SHOOT!" PETE CALLED in a fright. "It's me! Your son!" he added, as if his own pa might not own him.

"Pete? Show yourself!"

I watched from behind the trees as Pete rode forward to where the light from the lanterns and the campfires could better identify him. Mr. Harkness spat into the grass.

"I recollect telling you to stay home. Whose horse is that?"

"Mr. Bell's, sir."

"Get down from there."

Pete jumped down from the gelding as Mr. Moultray stepped over.

"Did you take that horse out of my stable, boy? Without my permission?"

Now Mr. Osterman got involved.

"Don't take a conniption fit, Bill. That horse as good as belongs to the Harknesses."

"That's right," Pete's father said, as though Mr.

Osterman had just reminded him of the fact. "It should go to Annette."

"The merry widow," someone said.

There was laughter at that, until Mr. Harkness told everyone present, "Shut your traps!" Such is Mr. Harkness's temper and physical might that they obeyed him—and quickly, too.

Mr. Osterman said, "You should be proud of the boy, Dave. It took gumption to follow us like that."

I remembered that Mr. Osterman had said something similar about me the morning we found Mr. Bell's body, and it gave me the courage to come out of my hiding place. Besides, now that Pete had been discovered with our horse, it was show myself or walk all the way back to Nooksack by myself in the dark.

"Well, lookie here," said Mr. Harkness as I stepped forward. "Mr. Gillies, this one belongs to you, does he not?"

Father, who had been resting against a fallen log paying scant attention to Pete and the horse, now looked over. It took him a moment to focus his eyes on me, and another to get over his disbelief at seeing me there. He got to his feet and came over to me slowly. I was aware that the other men were watching him, and I did not for one minute like their grinning expressions.

"I told you to stay home, George," Father said.

I replied, "I wanted to help catch the renegade, sir, and to make him pay for what he did to poor Mr. Bell."

I was showing him all the respect I could muster, just to prove to those men that he was a man worth respecting. But it seemed I only made matters worse, for Pete's father got a smirk on his face to end all.

"Looks like you got more backbone than your old man, son," said Mr. Harkness.

Without uttering a word in reply, my father turned away and went back to the log he had been leaning on. Part of me wanted to go over and sit with him, to show those laughing men that I was on his side, no matter what. But a bigger part of me—the part that wanted to see justice done—told me to stand with the posse. That's the part that won out. I went to warm my hands at a small campfire that some of the men had started, keeping close to Pete and his pa—ignoring my own father. I felt guilty, but angry, too. Sometimes Father takes being his own man too far.

AT THE APPOINTED TIME, the men mounted their horses and started north to Mr. York's farmhouse at Sumas Prairie. Pete and I were allowed to go with them, mostly because there was no longer the danger of the posse being attacked by a whole band of Indians. But we were told by Mr. Osterman to keep to the back of the group, because the things that would be happening were not suitable for boys our age to be witnessing up close.

Mr. Bell's horse had a short gait that made for a bumpy ride even at a walk, but I tried to think about the satisfaction of seeing the look on that Indian's face when at last we'd have him cornered—instead of how squished I felt behind Pete on that saddle. After the way the men had spoken to my father, I did not think it wise to push the point with Pete that it was my turn to be riding up front, lest I get some of the same treatment.

By about ten o'clock, we were getting close to Mr. York's farmhouse. Jack Simpson had not returned to us, which was taken as a sign that he had been allowed into the house by Mr. York and would unbolt the door for us once the household was asleep. At last we could see our destination by starlight, a fine two-story frame house that spoke to Mr. York's success. The yard was even fenced with white pickets, to keep the livestock out of Mrs. York's flower beds, I supposed. All was quiet—not so much as a dog barking. Mr. Osterman called the posse to a halt a good two hundred yards off.

"This is it," he said, his voice low. "It's now or never—our last chance to show Louie Sam American justice." He pulled his revolver out of its holster. "I need ten men to come inside with me."

Most of the men were eager to go into the house

with Mr. Osterman. Among the chosen few were Pete's pa, Mr. Moultray, and Mr. Breckenridge. My father was not among those who volunteered, nor was he asked. The only one of the leaders to stay back was little Mr. Hopkins, who, now that the plan was actually about to be hatched, seemed frightened by the whole business.

"Once we're inside the house," said Mr. Moultray, "the rest of you gather in the yard. Give them a show of our numbers, just in case Mr. York or the other constable has any ideas about keeping us from our purpose."

In the excitement, I suppose Mr. Moultray forgot about Pete and me, because no further mention was made of us being too young to witness what was about to happen. We waited with the other men, still on horseback, watching as Mr. Osterman and Mr. Moultray dismounted and led the party up through the white picket fence to the house and onto the veranda—rifles and revolvers at the ready. By the light of their lanterns, we could make out Mr. Osterman approaching the door and trying the latch. A second later, Mr. Osterman disappeared into the house, followed by the others. We saw their lantern light through the parlor window. I swear that barely a breath was taken by those of us left behind. We waited.

Suddenly, a woman was screaming—followed

by angry shouts. We couldn't be sure whether the shouting was coming from our men or from the Canadian constables, but nevertheless we took it as our cue. Spurring our horses, we rode as a pack up into the farmhouse yard, leaping the fence or crowding through the gate, whooping and hollering—making as much noise as we could to show the Canadian lawmen that we meant business. Pete and I joined in the hoopla, although we did not have the benefit of costumes and painted faces to boost the effect as the others did.

In a few moments, Dave Harkness appeared at the door, dragging with him into the yard a cowed and stumbling body, his hands cuffed behind his back. Mr. Osterman and Mr. Moultray were right behind them. A cry went up from the posse. We had him—we had the murderer!

Leaving Pete, I slipped off the horse's back and pushed my way through the pack to get a better look. The Indian was on his knees in the dirt with Mr. Harkness and Mr. Moultray leaning over him. Mr. Harkness pulled him to his feet. That's when I got my first good look at Louie Sam, as well as the shock of my life.

Louie Sam was just a boy, even younger than I.

CHAPTER NINE

LOUIE SAM WAS SMALL BUT broad-faced, his skin the
copper color of his people. His dark hair hung shaggy
and loose, not braided the way a brave would have
it. I wondered if he was too young to wear his hair
that way. The posse men jeered at him and called him
names as they gathered around him in the farmyard,
but he said nothing. The look on his face was some-
where between surly and terrified, though from the
way he shook, it seemed to me he was more scared
than angry. But he could well have been shaking from
the cold night, because the men had pulled him out of
the house the way I guess he had been sleeping, with
only his shirt and pants, his suspenders hanging loose
and no boots on his feet.

I remembered Pete saying he was struck by fear
the day of Mr. Bell's murder, seeing the evil look of
Louie Sam when he passed him on the Lynden road.
Pete was a couple of years older than Louie Sam, and
at least a head taller. I wondered, *What was it about
this Indian boy that had seemed so fearsome to Pete?*

There was nothing fearsome about him now. He was shrinking into himself, keeping his head bowed like he was expecting a beating. But at the same time, there was something about the way he held his back and shoulders, stiff and proud, that made it seem like he wasn't the least bit sorry for what he'd done to find himself in this situation.

Old Mr. York came out on the veranda, cussing at our men in a Scots brogue thicker than my father's. He was fit to be tied that guns had been pointed at his wife and daughter, who were presently under guard by one of our number in an upstairs room. The other constable, Steele, didn't seem so worked up as Mr. York. He was quiet and let Mr. York do the talking. When Jack Simpson slipped out of the house and rejoined us, Mr. York was madder than a wet hen.

"You! One of these border ruffians, are ye? I take ye into my house in the middle of the night, and this is the thanks I get?"

From his place on the veranda, Mr. York peered out into the posse that filled his yard, Mr. Steele at his side. Our numbers and our disguises seemed to make him think twice about his show of temper, because he cooled down a notch or two.

"What kind of cowards dress up in their wives' frocks?" he spat, but he lacked the fire he had spewed only a moment before.

Mr. Moultray spoke. "We've got no argument with

you. We came for the Indian. That's all."

Mr. York squinted into the darkness. "Is that you, Bill Moultray?"

It seemed to me that Louie Sam turned his head at the mention of Mr. Moultray's name.

"Take my advice, sir," said Mr. Osterman, "and mind your own business."

Mr. York looked at the Indian boy shivering in his yard, his hands bound behind his back with cuffs of metal.

"The Sumas won't like it," he said. "They handed him to my son-in-law because they were promised a fair trial."

"Don't you worry," answered Mr. Harkness. "We'll make sure he gets a fair trial."

There was spirited laughter and rumblings of agreement from the posse at that. The old man seemed to weigh his options—which were few and far between.

"Think about what you're doing, Bill," said Mr. York, addressing Mr. Moultray. Mr. Moultray stayed quiet, like he didn't want to give himself away again with his voice. "This isn't the South. We don't hang a body just for being colored."

It was the first time anybody had mentioned hanging since we arrived at Mr. York's. I peered over at Louie Sam to see his reaction, but he didn't flinch from keeping his head low and still—which made me think he didn't understand English too well.

"I don't recall anybody talking about hanging him," called Mr. Osterman. "We want him to face justice, that's all."

Mr. York waved away the posse with his hands, fed up with us.

"Take him then. Just be gone away from my house, the lot of ye, and off my land!"

A spare horse was led forward, one that was brought along for the purpose, and Louie Sam was lifted and placed upon its bare back, his hands still cuffed.

"We'll return the bracelets in the morning," Mr. Harkness told Mr. York.

With that, the posse left Mr. York's yard, led by Mr. Osterman and Mr. Moultray—who, I noticed, continued to hold his tongue. Mr. Harkness took up the reins of the pony that carried Louie Sam and pulled it along behind him. I went to climb aboard Mr. Bell's horse with Pete, but my father called to me.

"George," he said. "You ride with me."

I didn't argue, and climbed up into Mae's saddle behind him.

Now that I saw Louie Sam with my own eyes, saw that he was flesh and blood—saw that he was no more than a kid—the real purpose of the Nooksack Vigilance Committee was hitting home. *That boy is coming back to Nooksack to die,* I realized. I knew that from the start, I guess, but it was just a fact to me then—a matter that needed to be settled in the name of justice for Mr. Bell. Why did it feel so different now? Suddenly, I was having a hard time picturing the scene at Mr. Bell's place. How could a boy John's age march into that cabin and shoot the old man in the back of the head, in cold blood?

Something was niggling at me as we rode, like my brain was trying to tell me I'd missed something. Then all at once it came to me.

"He's wearing suspenders!"

Father turned his ear toward me. "What did you say?"

"Louie Sam. He's wearing suspenders. Those weren't his suspenders we found in the swamp."

Father said nothing for a few moments. I held on to him, feeling the muscles of his back working in rhythm with Mae. At last he spoke, keeping his voice very low.

"That doesn't mean anything. He could have found himself a second pair."

"But there's a chance he didn't. There's a chance those were somebody else's suspenders in the swamp. That somebody else was running away from Mr. Bell's cabin."

Father turned his head to me, so only I could hear. "Keep that to yourself."

"But it's evidence!" I said.

"Quiet!" he hissed.

"We have to tell them," I whispered in his ear.

"It's too late. They won't listen."

"But—"

"Enough!"

When my father says "enough," that's the end of it. I held my tongue, but my brain would not stop thinking. Everything had seemed so certain on the ride north. Now nothing was. Riding ahead of me in the darkness was the boy who murdered Mr. Bell, but maybe he didn't. If justice was what we were after, then surely justice meant knowing without a doubt that he was guilty. I took my father's point, though. Emotions were running high. My father was already suspected of soft resolve. This was not the time to mount a defense of Louie Sam, especially not coming from us Gillies. I decided that once we got Louie Sam back to the jail in Nooksack, I would go to Sheriff Leckie and tell him about the suspenders.

But after riding for not even an hour, the posse stopped in a clearing. We were less than halfway home. It seemed odd to me that the men would want to take a break, considering the seriousness of their business. Then a rider—the same Jack Simpson who'd entered Mr. York's house as our spy—came galloping past us in the opposite direction, going back up the Whatcom Trail from where we'd just come. Word filtered back through the ranks that Mr. Osterman and Mr. Moultray had sent him on a scouting mission, worried that maybe we were being followed by the Sumas—that they were riled that we'd taken one of their own, like Mr. York said they would be. If that was the case, we knew that every last man jack of us was in trouble, because the Canadian Indians were sure to outnumber us in a fight.

The men—including Father—checked that their firearms were loaded. I saw Pete nearby. I slipped off of Mae.

"George!" Father shouted.

"I'll be right back!" I told him.

I went over to Pete.

"I got something to tell you."

"What might that be?"

He was acting huffy, looking down on me from his borrowed saddle.

"I'm not sure that Louie Sam's the one that left that trail, the one we followed through the swamp."

"What are you talking about? Anybody with eyes can see that Indian is guilty as sin, Gillies."

The way Pete said our family name made me mad, like he thought we were less than other people—especially his people. To get back at him, I said, "What were you so scared of him for when you saw him on the Lynden road? He's only a boy."

Pete was about to spew something back at me, but at that moment Jack Simpson came galloping back

again—this time riding toward the head of the posse.
I forgot about Pete and started making my way up
front to find out what was going on. There I saw Louie
Sam, straddling the back of the pony, his hands still in
cuffs behind his back. He kept his gaze directed to the
ground but his back was straight. Jack Simpson was
telling the posse leaders that, as far as he could see,
the trail behind us was clear of Indians.

"That doesn't mean they won't be coming soon,"
Mr. Osterman observed.

"We should hand him over if they do," said Mr.
Hopkins, who looked smaller than ever, perched on
a horse that was too big for him. "Let the Canadians
put him on trial."

"That's not going to happen," declared Pete's pa.

"What are we waiting for?" said Mr. Osterman.
"Dave, where's that rope?"

Mr. Harkness took up a rope that was hanging in
a coil from the horn of his saddle. I felt my stomach
tighten. I glanced to Louie Sam, who didn't flinch.

Mr. Moultray pointed out, "We're still on the
Canadian side."

"So?"

"So if there's trouble about this, it'll fall under
Canadian law."

"If there's trouble about this," said Mr. Osterman,
"better it be on their side of the border, with us safe
on our side."

82

Other men spoke up, agreeing with Mr. Harkness and Mr. Osterman that they should get on with it. They meant to hang him, right here! A fever was building among the men. They were jeering at Louie Sam, calling for his blood. Louie Sam lifted his head at the commotion, but said nothing and showed no fear. I was certain now he couldn't understand much English—he couldn't know what was about to happen to him. Or if he did, he was the bravest person I'd ever seen.

"Look at him, dumb as a brute!" Mr. Harkness shouted.

I thought of speaking up about the suspenders, but I lost my chance among the rising calls for action. It was just like Father said—they wouldn't listen. There was no arguing with them now as they spurred each other on.

"Murdering dog!" called out Mr. Breckenridge.

Then he spat on the boy. Louie Sam looked up at that, his eyes fierce with hatred. Mr. Osterman rode up to a giant cedar with a thick branch eight feet off the ground.

"This'll do," he said. "Bring the rope."

Mr. Harkness trotted his horse up to Mr. Osterman. Mr. Osterman held his lantern up high to light the way for Mr. Harkness as he swung the rope once, then twice. On the third swing he tossed the rope. The noose dangled over the branch. Everyone fell silent at the sight of it. Mr. Harkness tied off the other end of the rope around the tree so the noose hung high, casting its shadow against the forest, while Mr. Breckenridge got down from his horse and grabbed hold of Louie Sam's right leg, pulling it around so the boy was sitting side saddle. He took a length of rope and bound his feet to match his hands. Then he led Louie Sam's pony under the tree branch.

Mr. Moultray rode up close to the pony. He got hold of the noose and yanked it over the boy's head, pulling the knot around so it was behind his ear. Now that Louie Sam got a close look at Mr. Moultray, he recognized him despite the black smudge and the streak of red war paint across his eyes. For the first and last time that night, Louie Sam spoke.

"Bill Moultray," he said.

Bill Moultray's eyes went wide with fright, like he'd been found out. The next thing I knew, he slapped the pony's flank, sending him running out from under the boy. And then Louie Sam was up in the air, fighting and struggling against the rope around his neck, even though his hands and feet were bound tight. He looked monstrous and terrified, twisting and writhing as he fought.

"For God's sake!" cried Mr. Hopkins. "Somebody put an end to him!"

Mr. Harkness raised his rifle.

"No shots!" called Mr. Osterman. "The Sumas might hear!"

Finally, Mr. Pratt rode up and raised the butt of his buffalo gun to Louie Sam's head. I looked away, but I couldn't stop my ears from hearing the blunt thud of wood meeting bone. When I looked up, Louie Sam was struggling no more. His body swung from the branch a few times, until at last he was still. His life was gone, but his fear was still there in his face for all to see, plain as day.

Everybody was silent. Then Mr. Harkness let out a whoop. A few others joined him trying to raise a cheer, among them Mr. Osterman and Mr. Breckenridge. Me, I didn't see what there was to cheer about. Mr. Moultray didn't seem to, either.

"Enough," he said.

He kicked his horse into a trot and headed down the trail toward home, not waiting for the other leaders. I made my way back to Father and Mae. Without a word, Father pulled me up behind him into the saddle. I kept my face buried in his back as he walked Mae past the hanging tree so I wouldn't have to see Louie Sam again. But I saw him in my mind, anyway. I will see him there forever.

CHAPTER TEN

As WE HEAD SOUTH ACROSS the border into the
Washington Territory, the men who had been
cheering and hollering the loudest for the end of
Louie Sam are silent. Once the deed was done, it was
like nobody wanted to think about it anymore. We
left him hanging from that cedar branch and we rode
away. We want to get back to our normal lives, to our
normal selves.

Everything is more complicated than I thought it
would be. I expected justice to feel good, but it feels
tight and cold in the pit of my stomach.

When we reach The Crossing, Mr. Moultray speaks
to us. His face is somber and weighted down, like he
doesn't feel in a celebrating mood any more than I do.
Or maybe he's just tired. I know I am. Mr. Moultray
tells the men that they did what needed to be done,
and that they should be proud. But the next thing he
says is that none of us should ever talk about what
happened—not to our families, not to the sheriff, not
to anyone. The Nooksack Vigilance Committee is

henceforth a secret brotherhood. How can you have it both ways? If we're supposed to be so proud of what we did to Louie Sam, then why are we keeping secrets about it?

FIRST LIGHT STARTS TO show above the trees to the east as Father, Mae, and I follow the track along Sumas Creek to our mill and our cabin. From a distance, we see chimney smoke above the trees. Why does Mam have a full fire going at such an hour, when normally she would just be rising? Father gives Mae a kick. She trots ahead a little, but quickly falls back into a walk—like us, worn out from the night's outing. Father kicks her harder.

"Get up!" he says, his voice crusty and thick. He hasn't used it since we left the hanging spot.

Gypsy comes running to meet us, barking in a fury of excitement. When we leave the trees and our cabin comes into sight, we get another surprise. A woman is outside, pitching water from a bucket onto the ground. When she turns around, I see that she's Agnes, the Nooksack squaw who was Bill Hampton's Indian wife.

"Agnes!" my father calls to her. "Where's my wife?"

Mae has picked up her pace, eager now that she knows her feed is close by. Agnes straightens up and waits for Mae to trot up to the cabin and for Father to rein her in before speaking. Her English is not good, despite living with a white man for all those years. She relies mostly on Chinook to make herself understood.

"*Bébe yuk'-wa,*" she says.

There's the cry of a newborn from inside the cabin, making her meaning clear enough—while we were gone, the new baby arrived! Father leaps down from the saddle and tells me to see to Mae, then he barrels into the house. Agnes follows him into the cabin, slow and easy, like she lives here. Anxious as I am to see my new brother or sister, I feed and water Mae and Ulysses. I see from the way the two cows are shifting in their stall that they need milking, so I do that, too. After riding all night and being alone with too many thoughts, it feels good to keep my hands busy.

By the time I go inside, the new baby already has a name. He is to be called Edward, after Mam's father. Teddy for short. The baby and Mam are both asleep in my parents' bed, behind a curtain they have rigged for privacy. I go around the curtain and take a peek. Teddy is bundled in Mam's arms, looking no different to my eyes from any of my other brothers or sisters when they were born. I let the curtain fall and step as quietly as I can over to the table near the stove, where Annie is pouring tea for Father out of the old china pot that Mam brought from England. The boys come out from the back room, wiping sleep from their eyes. I tell John that he should have done the milking. John says he was up half the night bringing in firewood for the stove while Teddy got born. Father shushes us, so as not to wake Mam. It's strange to see Agnes taking Mam's place at the stove, a full-blooded Indian stirring the porridge just like a white woman would. Her face is cut deep with wrinkles, but she can't be that old.

"We owe you thanks, Agnes," my father says quietly. He takes a long sip of the tea, even though it's scalding hot.

Agnes nods toward John. *"Man mam'-ook cháh-ko ni-ka."* She seems sad, even when she smiles.

"She means I went for her," says John. "When Mam's pains started, I didn't know what else to do—or when you'd be back."

We all fall silent at that. I wonder if Agnes knows where we were last night, and what we were doing. She shows no curiosity, but John does. He whispers to me, "So what happened? Did you get him?"

He says it with such eagerness that I want to smack him. I wish I could tell him right there and then about how complicated it is, but Mam is sleeping—and it doesn't feel right to talk about Louie Sam in front of a native woman.

"I'll tell you later," I say.

Father gives me a sharp look and I remember that we're not supposed to say anything at all. He takes another sip of tea. I take a seat at the table, and thank Agnes kindly when she puts a bowl of porridge in front of me.

It's Thursday, but nobody even talks about going to school today. After breakfast, Father heads straight away down to the mill. Agnes stays and kneads some dough so we'll have fresh bread for the evening meal. Mam wakes up and Agnes brings her a bowl of yesterday's bread softened in some warm milk. From behind the curtain on the other side of the room, I listen to Mam and Agnes talking in soft voices, but I can't make out what they're saying. Female talk, oohing and aahing over the new baby. I suppose it's the same in any language. At the table, Isabel is singing softly to her dolly, pretending that she has a new baby, too. Annie's peeling potatoes. Everybody's calm. It's nice.

Once the bread is baked, Agnes says she's going back home, to the shack she and her sons built in the woods a half mile up Sumas Creek, after they had to move out of the ferryman's house at The Crossing when Mr. Hampton died. Without asking, she takes two of the fresh loaves with her.

I go into the back room and lie down. I am so bone weary that I expect I could sleep standing up, but the minute I close my eyes I see Louie Sam hanging from that cedar, and the fear in his face. I open my eyes to make him go away and feel my heart racing. John comes into the room.

"Tell me what happened," he says.

"We're not supposed to talk about it," I reply.

"Says who?"

"Says Mr. Moultray."

"Did you get Louie Sam?"

"I can't say."

"You *did* get him, didn't you? Where is he now? Did they bring him to the jail in Nooksack?"

I look at him. Can he really be that dumb?

"He's not in any jail," I say.

John studies me for a minute, and then he understands.

"So you lynched him."

I know the word, but I haven't heard anyone use it in connection with Louie Sam. All the talk I've heard has been about justice and vigilance. *Lynched*. It's a rash word, harsher somehow than *hanged*. But it's what happened.

"Yeah," I say.

John watches my face again, and his own face changes. Some of the eagerness goes out of his expression.

"Did he put up a fight?"

"No ... Yes, but only at the end."

"Well, did he say anything in his own defense?"

"He hardly said anything. He was too scared."

"Hah! The coward."

"He wasn't a coward," I tell him. Then I add, because it seems like something that's important to know, "He was just a kid."

"How old a kid?"

"Thirteen. Fourteen at most."

This takes John aback. Then he says, "A murderer's a murderer."

I don't have a reply to that. I say, "Let me sleep."

CHAPTER ELEVEN

I WAKE UP AT NOON, edgy with the trembles of a bad
dream. And then I remember it wasn't a dream. All
of us are worn out, between Father and me riding
all night and the baby getting born. At noon we sit
around the table eating cheese and bread, staying quiet
so as not to wake Mam and the baby. None of us has
much to say, anyway.

In the afternoon, Tom Breckenridge's father brings
grain to be milled, but he doesn't stay much longer
than it takes for Father and me to grind the single
sack of wheat he's brought with him. I open the sluice
gate to let the water rush in from the wheel and drive
the runner stone, while Father empties the wheat
into the hopper. Then I hurry down to the meal floor
to collect the flour in the sack as it comes down the
chute. From upstairs, I can hear Mr. Breckenridge
repeating to Father what Mr. Moultray told us at The
Crossing about keeping quiet—as though he thinks
Father needs reminding. I wonder if the real purpose
of Mr. Breckenridge's visit is to deliver that message.

Friday morning outside the school, while we're waiting for Miss Carmichael to ring the bell, Pete refuses to speak to me, except to tell me that we Gillies are Indian lovers because Father spoke up in favor of letting Louie Sam stand trial. John and I deny it hotly, but Tom Breckenridge says it's true—he heard the same thing from his pa. I think it's curious how Mr. Breckenridge told Tom what happened, after making a special trip to our place to warn Father to keep quiet. Tom says that as Mr. Bell's closest neighbors, it could just as easily have been them that Louie Sam attacked. Tom counts himself lucky that he and his family are still alive.

"My pa says the only good Indian is a dead Indian," Tom proclaims to the whole schoolyard. "We won't be safe until every last one of them is wiped out."

Pretty soon, it seems that Pete and Tom have got the whole school agreeing with them about us being Indian lovers. Adding to our reputation is the fact that it was Agnes rather than a proper settler's wife who helped bring my baby brother into the world. I try to explain to Pete and Tom that Agnes was closest at hand to our cabin, and that John didn't know what else to do but fetch her, with Father and me gone and Mam crying out that the baby was coming and coming fast. But nothing I say matters.

Pete is busy turning himself into some kind of hero, boasting to Abigail Stevens and the other girls about how he rode with the men on some very important business. He's stepping around the vow we all took not to say anything. But seeing as how just about everybody's father rode with the posse, everybody knows what happened, anyway, except for the lurid details—which Pete is pleased to provide, whispering them to the girls in a corner of the schoolyard.

After Miss Carmichael calls us inside, Abigail comes up to me in the cloakroom.

"Why are you letting Pete take all the attention, George?"

"He can have it," I tell her.

"You know what he's saying about you, don't you? He says you and your pa were cowards out there."

"He's a liar," I say.

"Then you better let folks know that," she replies.

Lately, Abigail seems more like a woman than a girl—and not just because her figure has rounded out. There's a matter-of-factness about her, like she's annoyed the other kids don't see the way things are in the grown-up world as clearly as she does. Abigail has always been smart at school. Also, she has pretty eyes.

"We were sworn not to talk about what happened," I tell her.

"Seems you're the only one keeping that promise. My pa told my ma all about it. He said he thought your pa had a good point, about letting that Indian have his day in court."

"Then why didn't your pa speak up?" I say.

"How should I know, George? Was I there? And don't go raising your voice to me when I'm trying to help you."

Outside, there is a sudden hullabaloo—shouting and hollering. Those of us who are indoors hurry out to the schoolyard to see what's the matter. By the time Abigail and I get there, a crowd three deep has circled around two boys flying fists at each other. The crowd—girls as well as boys—is egging them on, sounding just like the posse did in the minutes before Louie Sam died.

I push my way through to the front, and I see two things. The first is Pete, watching the fight with a stupid grin on his face. He's also leading the cheer. The second thing I see is that one of the boys is my brother, John, and the other is Jimmy Bell. Jimmy's half a head taller than John and has got the advantage of weight on his side. But John is a wiry scrapper and will never give up, which I know from wrassling with him myself.

Jimmy gets John in a headlock with his left arm and starts punching his face with his right fist.

"Give it to him, Jimmy!" yells Tom Breckenridge, standing at Pete's side.

I'm itching to run in and pull Jimmy off of my brother, but I know that if I do, John will never forgive me for saving him like that in front of everybody.

Now Abigail is shouting, "Stop it, Jimmy! You're hurting him!"

Miss Carmichael is on the front porch of the schoolhouse, blowing her whistle for them to stop—to no effect whatsoever. John's face is bloodied, his nose broken for sure. Annie and Will are across the circle from me.

"Let go of him!" Annie calls to Jimmy. Then she sees me across the way. "George, make him stop!"

But John manages to hook Jimmy's leg with his foot. Jimmy falls hard on his back and John is on top of him, his small fists pounding into Jimmy's big face—giving him back the beating that he just took. Now that John is winning, it's safe for me to mix in. I hold off for a second or two, though, to give John his due revenge. I look over to Pete, thinking he might be wanting to rescue Jimmy, his more-or-less stepbrother. Pete has stopped shouting for blood, but I see he's smiling a little—like he's just as pleased to see Jimmy being pummeled as he was to see John in that spot a minute ago.

I make my move. Striding forward, I grab hold of John by both his arms and drag him off of Jimmy.

"That's enough!" I say.

John struggles to get free from me, but I can tell it's mostly for show. He's had enough. There's blood running out of his nose, and he'll have two shiners. The kids around us step back, loosening the circle they formed to watch the fight—those who a moment ago wanted a ringside view suddenly wanting to melt away into the background as Miss Carmichael descends from the porch, blowing her whistle. Her voice is tight and high when she demands to know, "What in heaven's name is going on here?"

"He called my ma a whore!" Jimmy cries out, staggering to his feet and pointing at John.

"Only because you called Agnes one!" shouts John right back.

"She's just an Indian," says Jimmy. "She doesn't count."

John can't keep quiet. "Agnes is nice! She helped Mam!"

I think to myself, *There's our reputation as Indian lovers—set in stone.*

Abigail says, "Everybody knows your ma's a whore, Jimmy."

Miss Carmichael is scandalized. "Abigail Stevens!"

"Well, it's true."

I notice that Pete Harkness gives Abigail no argument whatsoever in defense of Mrs. Bell.

Miss Carmichael kicks John out of school for the rest of the day for fighting, but not Jimmy because she says his father just died and he deserves special consideration. But each boy is sporting a bloody nose, so she winds up sending them both home, anyway.

John is in no condition to be walking all that distance alone, so I tell Miss Carmichael I'm going with him, and Will can walk Annie home later. To make up for missing another whole day of school, Miss Carmichael makes me take home a book by Ralph Waldo Emerson, her favorite writer, and tells me to memorize one of his poems for Monday.

Mam, barely on her feet after having the baby, gets upset with John. His nose has swollen up fiercely by the time we get home and she says it will never look right again. But when she learns what the fight was about, that John was defending Agnes, she is more forgiving. She soaks a rag in hot water and makes a poultice for him to hold over his nose and his eyes.

Father has little to say about the fight, other than that John should have kept his fists higher to protect his face. Since Wednesday night, he's been quiet, preferring to spend most of his time alone in the mill instead of with the rest of us in the cabin. He barely pays attention to Teddy. With Father spending all his time in the mill, the chores fall to John and me. That's fine with me. It feels good to keep busy, and I like spending the rest of the day away from people.

Late in the afternoon, before John and I have to give the cows their evening milking, I settle myself in a quiet corner of the shed and open the book by Mr. Emerson to a poem called "Nature." It's full of fancy language, the gist of which is that God is all around

us. That seems like a wrong-headed idea to me—
everybody knows God is in Heaven. Isn't Nature what
leads us astray, like the snake tempting Eve with the
apple? I thought Nature was what we sinners were put
on earth to overcome, but here this poem seems to say
that Nature is its own kind of god. I wish I could talk
with Father about what it means, but remembering
the scowl he wore when he came into the house
for the noon meal warns me against it. He isn't even
talking to Mam, not very much.

It rains all day Saturday. After supper, when
Teddy and the younger kids have gone to bed and
Father has taken a lantern back down to the mill, I
find a moment alone with Mam. She's sitting in the
rocking chair we brought all the way from England.
Her eyes are closed, but I can tell she's awake from the
way she's rocking herself ever so gently.

"Will you listen to this poem I had to learn?" I
ask her.

She opens her eyes, so weary that I think she might
have been sleeping after all.

"Aye, Georgie. Let me hear it."

I begin reciting, but when I get to the part—

For Nature listens in the rose
And hearkens in the berry's bell

To help her friends, to plague her foes,
And likewise God she judges well.

—I stop. Mam's eyes have been closed again, her face soft while she's been listening. Now she comes back to the world.

"Is that the end of it?"

"No. There's more."

"Why did you stop?"

"It doesn't seem right, Nature judging God. God made Nature. Only God can judge."

"I suppose," she says, all dreamy.

It surprises me that she isn't troubled the way I am, she being the one who insists we go to church every Sunday.

"But it's wrong," I tell her.

"It's just a poem, George. A nice poem. You learned it well." She eases herself up from the rocking chair. You can tell she's stiff and sore. "Time to get to bed now, for both of us."

She takes a candle and moves slowly toward her bed, pulling the curtain across behind her. I watch through the gap as she reaches into Teddy's cradle and pulls a blanket up over him. In the candlelight, her eyes shine and her smile is full of wonder. One thing I'll say for Mr. Emerson's poetry: Mam sure seems to like it.

CHAPTER TWELVE

ON SUNDAY MORNING, NEITHER Mam nor Father seems to remember about Sunday school, and we children are not disposed to remind them. The day starts gray and cool, nothing like the previous Sunday, the day we found Mr. Bell's body. Can it be that only a week has gone by? It seems like it all happened to somebody else, like in a story.

I'm splitting wood in the yard when, late in the morning, we have a visitor. It's Agnes's son, Joe Hampton. Agnes has sent him over with a brace of quail, wanting to trade them for eggs and a quantity of flour. When Joe sees John's shiners, he tells Mam there's a paste his ma makes from yellow flowers to bring down bruises and he offers to fetch some. But before he does that, Mam insists on giving him a bowl of the barley soup she's cooking for our lunch, which he eats outside, leaning against the paddock fence.

Joe is a few years older than I am. His hair is long and wild and he's dark-skinned like an Indian, but his eyes are blue from his father. He speaks English

like a white man, but with a lilt he got from the way
his mother's people talk. As he eats, he watches me
work, and I half watch him, feeling awkward about his
presence. I'm mindful of having recently been called
an Indian lover, and of now having one dining right
here on my doorstep.

"You're George," he says, after a few spoonfuls of
the soup.

"That's right."

I set another log on the chopping stump.

"I heard you rode with them the other night."

This to me seems disrespectful, an Indian
questioning me about my business.

"I don't know what you're talking about," I say.

I bring the ax down on the log, but my aim is
off and instead of splitting it, I send it flying off the
stump. I wish this hadn't happened in front of Joe. As
I bend over to pick up the log, he tells me, "People are
talking. The Sumas are worked up about it."

I say, "The Sumas ought to acknowledge the fact
that one of them is a murderer."

"What murderer would that be?" he asks.

"You know what murderer."

He won't let it go. "That's just it. Louie Sam talked
to his ma. He told her he didn't do it."

This hits me. For one thing, I never thought about
Louie Sam having a mother. For another, I've got
that niggling feeling working at me again, making

me wonder whether Father was right, whether the Nooksack Vigilance Committee should have let Louie Sam stand trial. Joe Hampton fixes me with a look, like he's reading something in my face. I turn away quickly.

"Of course that's what his ma would say," I tell him. "Anyway, the Sumas are just protecting their own."

"We don't abide outlaws any more than you whites do. Look at Louie's pa. When Justice Campbell showed the Sumas chiefs enough evidence, they handed him over for murder."

"For a Nooksack, you seem to know an awful lot about the Sumas," I remark.

"Louie Sam was my cousin," he says. "His ma and my ma had the same *chope*—grampa."

I don't want to know that. I don't want to hear any more about Louie Sam, or about his family. I split another log, cleanly down the middle this time—hoping Joe will take the message that this conversation is at an end.

"Thursday morning, Justice Campbell showed up at the Sumas village to tell the chiefs that a lynch mob had come up from the American side to take Louie away from Thomas York's house." I keep chopping wood, pretending not to listen. "Big Charlie and Sam Joe went with Justice Campbell to track the mob down the Whatcom Trail until just before the border. That's where they found Louie, still hanging where he'd been left the night before."

My limbs cease to function for the moment and I have to let the ax rest on the block. Joe Hampton knows he's gotten to me. He lets me sweat for a little before saying, "But I suppose you know all about that."

I'm done listening to him. I stack up the chopped wood in my arms and walk past him, heading for the cabin. Before I get to the door, Joe decides he's got something else to tell me.

"The People of the River are coming to Sumas from all over."

"*What* people?"

"The People of the River. The *Stó:lō*. We're deciding what should be done to avenge my cousin's death."

"You don't avenge justice," I tell him. But I'm blowing smoke, and he knows it.

"Let me tell you about justice, the *Stó:lō* way. Among our people, if you kill one of our kin, then one of *your* kin has to die. Doesn't matter who. Any white man will do."

From the look in his eyes, I get the feeling he would be satisfied if that somebody was me, here and now. But in the next second he's friendly again, telling me to thank Mam for the soup. He sets the bowl on the fence post and I watch him as he heads away down the path toward the creek. Then I go inside the cabin and stack the wood by the stove. I'm wondering exactly how many Indians are gathering at Sumas, and whether the Nooksack on our side of the border will stand with them—and how far the lot of them intend to go in pursuit of what they call justice. I'm wondering how safe my family will be if Louie Sam's kin decide they're coming across the border to settle the score.

I HAVE TO TELL FATHER that the Indians are gathering, that they're thinking about attacking. I head down to the mill, but he's not where I expect to find him, oiling the driveshaft or cleaning the mill stones as he would normally be doing when the mill is idle. It's cold in the mill, and silent—except for the scream of gulls circling over our pond. Then I hear a tinkling noise outside. I open one of the shutters on the window, and there's my father, perched on the ledge beside the waterwheel— doing his business into the pond. I decide to wait until he's done to talk to him. But I'm too late. He's seen me leaning out the window.

"What in damnation do you want?!" he thunders.

I have seen my father drunk only once before, when the baby girl that was born after Annie and before Isabel died. He was sad and quiet then. He's angry now.

"Leave me alone!" he yells. "All of ye leave me the hell alone!"

I pull my head back inside so fast I knock it against the jamb. I see a liquor jug on his workbench, just like the jugs that Pete Harkness's pa brings home from Doc Barrow's Five Mile Roadhouse, and from which

Pete and I stole a nip once or twice. I pull out the stopper and my eyes sting from the fumes. The jug is almost empty. I'm tempted to pour the rest of it out onto the floor, but I'm afraid of what Father will do in his present state if he finds out.

I think about telling Mam about what Joe Hampton said, but it would be wrong to worry her right now, when she's busy with the new baby. I decide to keep my fears about the Indians attacking to myself for now.

When I return to the cabin, everybody is at sixes and sevens. Annie and Isabel are squabbling because Isabel won't mind Annie and take her nap. Teddy won't stop crying, and Mam is fretting about what's gotten into Father just when she needs him the most. I daren't tell her where he is, nor what condition he's in. This being Sunday, I have a notion that I should step up in his place and read something calming from the Bible to all of them, but when I open the Good Book and start reading out loud from Deuteronomy, these are the first words I find:

So shalt thou put away the guilt of innocent blood from among you, when thou shalt do that which is right in the sight of the Lord.

"What's wrong, George?" says Mam. "Keep reading."

"I can't," I tell her.

Because when I read those words, all I can think about is Louie Sam.

Chapter Thirteen

Monday morning, Teddy is running a fever. Mam is worried enough to want to take him into town to see Dr. Thompson. But Father says he won't go into town. He tells me to hitch Ulysses and Mae to the wagon and for me to take them, meaning I will miss yet another day of school—which is fine with me, given the name-calling I suffered on Friday and the heathen poem Miss Carmichael expects me to recite today.

Our wagon is really just an open cart that we use for carrying supplies. The weather is drizzling and cold. Mam settles herself on the bench and holds the baby bundled against her in a blanket. Father puts an oilskin over her head and shoulders. For a moment, I think he's going to tell me to move aside, that he will take Mam into town in my place. For a moment, I think Mam will ask him to. But neither one of them says anything. I whip the reins, not too hard, and tell Ulysses and Mae to geddup. Father stands in the rain watching us go.

Mam stays silent while we ride, but I can feel

her worry. I know she's thinking about the little girl between Annie and Isabel. She called that baby Marie. She died when she was just a few days older than Teddy is now. I know she's worrying about how she's going to pay Dr. Thompson, too, because with customers seeming to spurn us and our mill all week—and with Father making visits to Doc Barrow's Roadhouse—the jar in which Father keeps his earnings has been emptier than usual.

DR. THOMPSON'S OFFICE IS at the back of an apothecary he runs on Nooksack Avenue, across from the new hotel that went up last year. The rain has turned the street to mud that sucks at the wagon's wheels and slows Ulysses and Mae down. It seems that we will be trapped forever in this jostling cart with the misty rain coming at us sideways, but at last we're there. I take hold of Teddy while Mam climbs down from the wagon. He feels like a feather in my arms. He mewls and cries, wanting Mam. I'm relieved when I put him back into her arms. She tells me to come into the apothecary with her out of the rain, because she doesn't need two sick children on her hands.

The shop has a whole wall of shelves filled with bottles and jars of various sizes, containing all sorts of powders and liquids. Mrs. Thompson is behind the counter, weighing something that looks like dried ragweed on a scale. She's older than Mam and on the ample side. Well fed, as Father would say.

"Good morning," she says, without taking her eyes off the scale. When she finally looks up at Mam, she sees in her face that something is seriously wrong. She comes around to our side of the counter and takes the baby from her. Peeking under the blanket, she coos to him.

"What a fine boy you have, Mrs. Gillies," she says. But you can tell that she's just trying to make Mam feel that everything is going to be all right—when, in fact, she thinks that Mam has good reason to be concerned. "Bring the baby and sit by the stove, dear. Dr. Thompson is with a patient. He shouldn't be very much longer."

Mam thanks Mrs. Thompson and does as she says. There are two chairs, but I don't feel right about sitting in the other one, dripping wet as I am and muddy from the splatter kicked up by the wagon's wheels. Besides which, it's too hot beside the stove, and I don't like the medicine smell that fills the room. Anyway, all the time we were traveling from our farm, I was forming an intention of my own.

"I'm going to see to Mae and Ulysses," I say.

"Don't be standing out in the rain," Mam warns me.

I go outside and check briefly that Mae and Ulysses are hitched firmly to the post so that I won't have told Mam an out-and-out lie, then I keep walking across the street to the new hotel.

The Nooksack Hotel is as fancy as it comes in these parts, three stories tall with a spiral staircase winding upward from the lobby to the rooms. Mr. Hopkins, the manager, is behind a long raised counter. He peers at me funny through his eyeglasses when I walk in. I nod to him like I'm here on important business, which I am. I'm headed to a small office off the other side of the sitting area—the telegraph office.

Since Father doesn't want to hear about the Sumas Indians coming together just across the border, I have decided it's my duty as a citizen of Whatcom County to tell somebody in authority about what Joe Hampton told me. Mr. Moultray would be my first choice, but he is located another two miles away at The Crossing. Mr. Osterman is closer at hand, here in town. The door is closed, but through the glass panel I can see him at his desk with his back to me, and I can hear him tap-tapping away at his machine.

The telegraph works by sending little bursts of electricity down a wire strung from pole to pole to Ferndale, then Bellingham Bay, and from there all the way to California and beyond. The electricity is made inside a battery—a glass jar filled with copper and zinc and water that somehow starts a current. Then the operator uses a key to transmit the bursts of electricity in a code of dots and dashes. The code stands for the alphabet. For instance, in Morse code, the letter A is one dot followed by one dash, the letter B is one dash and three dots, and so on. I don't know them all, though. At the receiving end, there's another telegraph operator who understands the code and copies down the message that's being sent, letter by letter.

I know all this because Miss Carmichael once invited Mr. Osterman to the school to tell us about his job. It seemed to me to be about the best job a fellow could have, sitting at a fine desk all day sending and receiving important messages. It's a job that earns respect, not the least because it's modern and scientific.

When Mr. Osterman stops tapping at the little black key and sits back in his chair, I knock on the door. I guess I've startled him, because he jumps a bit. But when he sees who it is, he waves me inside. He seems in a hurry though, like he doesn't have time to talk to me.

"What can I do for you, George?" he says.

He straightens the papers on his desk while he talks. He keeps his office neat and tidy, like his trimmed moustache and his freshly laundered clothes.

"There's something you need to know, Mr. Osterman."

"Oh? What might that be?"

"Joe Hampton says the Sumas are getting together. They're thinking about getting even, about attacking, because of—" I remember in the nick of time Mr. Moultray telling us not to speak about what happened.

"Because," I say, knowing he'll catch my drift.

Of all things, Mr. Osterman smiles.

"Does he now?" he says, acting like there's nothing in the world to be concerned about.

"Joe says their *tillicums* are coming from all up and down the Fraser River. He says …" I stop myself from speaking the forbidden name. "He says the boy told his mother that he was innocent."

This last piece of information makes Mr. Osterman's smile vanish. His brow furrows. His hands stop tidying the papers on his desk.

"He was lying, of course," I add quickly, mindful of the poor reputation we Gillies have acquired of late, and wanting to show him that I am on the right side of things.

"Who else have you told this to?" he asks.

"Nobody, sir."

"See that you keep it that way. The last thing we need is a lot of scare talk."

"But, sir, they intend to kill one of us. Joe ought to know. He's kin to Louie Sam—" I spoke the name! "The boy," I say in a hurry, correcting myself, "he was some kind of cousin to Joe."

Mr. Osterman gets up from his chair and steps toward me, looking me in the eye.

"Listen to me carefully, George. I know you want what's best for your neighbors and for your family. I know you want to keep them safe."

"Yes, sir."

"So don't go around spreading that dead Indian's lies about what happened. It just confuses people. Makes the Sumas think they got a case, when they got none. Tell your pa not to start spreading stories, either."

"But the attack—"

"They won't attack. I happen to know that the Canadian authorities are at that Sumas gathering at this very moment, talking them out of it." He nods toward the telegraph key. "Nothing happens around here that I don't know about. Now you get on to school, or wherever you're supposed to be."

He turns his back to me and sits down at his desk. I know he wants me out of there, but there's another reason I've come to see him. I've been thinking that maybe there's a way I can earn a little money to help pay Dr. Thompson.

"Mr. Osterman?"

"What is it?"

"Are you still looking for help?"

He turns around in his chair.

"Help with what?" he says.

He's irritated, and it rattles me.

"Help repairing the telegraph line."

"What are you talking about, George?"

"Like you were going to hire Louie Sam for."

My voice cracks as I say his name. I did it again!

Mr. Osterman's brow darkens like a gathering storm. I feel like a fool. I feel like running out of here before Mr. Osterman's temper explodes in my direction. But the strange thing is, all of a sudden Mr. Osterman stops being mad. He's friendly and nice.

"Thanks for the offer, George, but when I took a good look at the line that day, I realized we can get by until the summer. That's why there wasn't any work for …" He doesn't say the boy's name.

"But … you said you turned him away because you didn't like the look of him."

At that, his temper flares. He raises his voice. "Don't tell me what I said!"

I feel myself go red. I'm standing there like a fool, not knowing what to say. Then he calms down a little and tells me, "I was mistaken about needing to hire that boy. I only regret that poor Mr. Bell paid the price. Go on now," he says. "Git!"

I head back through the hotel lobby and go outside, keeping my eyes to the ground, burning with embarrassment. Pride goeth before a fall. I went into the telegraph office all puffed up with my big news, and I'm coming out feeling like an idiot. Why did I think that anything Joe Hampton had to say was worth passing on to somebody like Mr. Osterman? Why did I ever bring up repairing the line? But I could have sworn that Mr. Osterman told Sheriff Leckie that he sent Louie Sam away because he was ill-tempered. I don't remember him saying anything about him changing his mind and deciding there was no work for him, after all. I must have heard it all wrong.

It's raining harder now. Outside the hotel, there's a small man in a long canvas coat tying off a horse at the hitching post, his face hidden under a wide-brimmed hat. I turn my eyes away so that if it's somebody else important, he won't see me here. That's when I get a good look at the horse. It's Mr. Bell's gelding, the one that Pete and I rode up to Canada. Now I can't help myself from looking to see the man who's riding him. Only it isn't a man. It's Mrs. Bell—Annette—Pete's more-or-less stepmother. I guess somebody decided the horse should go to her. She looks me straight in the eye and smiles.

"Howdy, George," she says, with that Australian twang of hers. Her boldness comes across as unseemly. "Where have you been hiding yourself?" she asks me.

I stumble for a reply. "Nowhere, ma'am." Then, "I have to fetch my mother."

I reach the middle of Nooksack Avenue before I stop and glance back. I can see Mrs. Bell through the telegraph office window as she goes in to talk with Mr. Osterman. She's heated up about something, pointing out the window. Mr. Osterman looks outside—directly at me! The next thing I know, he's outside on the board-walk in his shirtsleeves, despite the rain coming down.

"George!" he calls to me. "On second thought, there's no reason to wait on those repairs until summer. Come see me around noon on Saturday. I'll get you started. How does a dollar and two bits a day sound?"

It sounds like the best thing that's happened in a long, long time. My heart takes a leap, I'm so excited.

"I'll be here!" I tell him. "Thanks, Mr. Osterman!"

"You're welcome," he says. "Come prepared to work hard, now."

"I will!"

I head over to meet Mam at the doctor's office, suddenly walking on air. I must be in Mr. Osterman's good books, after all, or he wouldn't have given me the job. Maybe now we Gillies can start living down our reputation as Indian lovers. Maybe now we can all get back to the way things were, before.

When I walk into the drug store, Mrs. Thompson is behind the counter handing Mam a bottle of Dr. Thompson's special patented medicine to help ease Teddy's fever. Mam has to ask Mrs. Thompson if she can pay for it next week, and Mrs. Thompson says all right. She's nice about it, but I know Mam hates having to ask. Once we're settled in the wagon and headed back out of town, I tell Mam not to worry, that soon I'll have the money to settle our account.

"And how might that be?" she asks.

"Mr. Osterman's paying me to check the telegraph

line," I reply. I'm so excited I could burst. But instead of being pleased she looks wearier still, like now she has one *more* thing to worry about. "What's wrong?" I ask. "I thought you'd be happy."

"I am, George. I am. Just be careful how you tell Father," she says.

"Don't you see, Mam?" I tell her. "The fact he gave me the job means he's forgiven Father. Now everybody will be friends with us again."

I have seldom heard my mother speak in anger, but it bursts from her now.

"Your father needs forgiving from God, and sometimes from me," she says, "but never from those hooligans!"

Hooligans! And not a word about me finding a paying job. I thought she would be pleased.

"They're not hooligans," I tell her, "any more than Father and I are!"

"You talk like you're proud of what happened to that boy," she hisses, wrapping her shawl tighter around the baby as though she needs to protect him from me.

For a moment I can't speak. I don't know if I can keep my voice steady.

"I'm not proud of it," I say at last, and my voice breaks just as I feared.

I'm aware of her looking over at me, but I keep my eyes straight ahead to where the motion of Mae's and

Ulysses's hindquarters is blurred by tears. She reaches out her hand and squeezes my arm.

"You're a good boy, George," she tells me. "I know you're a good boy."

I wipe my nose on my sleeve, and Mam doesn't remind me not to. I'm grateful for the drizzle that disguises the wet running down my cheeks.

BY THE NEXT MORNING, the tonic has made Teddy's fever go down, but he's still not feeding right. He sleeps all the time. Babies are supposed to sleep a lot, but Mam says they should wake up hungry and yelling for food, which Teddy does not. She is worn out with worrying. If Father is worried about Teddy, he doesn't show it the way Mam does. I think I know why. Speaking for myself, I am not attached to Teddy the same way I am to my other brothers and sisters. If he's going to die, I don't want to feel bad, the way I did with Baby Marie.

FIRST THING AT SCHOOL ON Tuesday, Miss Carmichael makes me recite that poem by Mr. Emerson she made me learn—in front of the entire class. Pete and Tom snicker, but Abigail tells them to hush up, and they do. On Wednesday, the boys invite me to play catch with them at the lunch break, like they normally would. The mill stays quiet all week, though, so maybe we Gillies haven't been completely forgiven like I'd hoped.

But it's been a mild winter and the farmers are busy getting a head start on their spring wheat. Father has started ploughing, too, which keeps him occupied and improves his mood. I mind what Mam said and wait for the right moment to tell him about me working for Mr. Osterman.

I'm in the shed milking on Thursday evening when Father comes in to hang up the plough for the night. I watch him take handfuls of oats from a sack and put them in a feed bag.

"Ulysses is getting a treat tonight," I say.

"Aye, he's earned it. We finished the lower field up to the creek."

"That's good."

Father is on his way out of the barn with the feed bag, whistling softly. This seems as good a time as any.

"I got a job," I say. I keep pulling on the cow's udders. He stops, turns back. I look up at him and tell him, "With Mr. Osterman."

He studies me for a long moment, but he isn't mad. Not yet, at least.

"What gave you cause to speak to Mr. Osterman?"

"I went on Monday when Mam and I were to town, to tell him what Joe Hampton told me about the Sumas attacking us."

He peers at me.

"About *what*?"

"Joe says the Sumas are gathering … on account

of what happened. But it's all right. Mr. Osterman said not to worry about it, that he knows from the telegraphs coming through the line that the Canadians have got the situation under control."

"And why did you not think to tell your own father about this before telling Mr. Osterman?"

"I tried," I say, not wanting to tell him why I did not succeed.

I wait for his anger, but it doesn't come. For a moment, he seems unable to look at me. I tell him, "Mr. Osterman said not to tell anybody about the Sumas lest it starts a scare. He told me to tell you the same."

"Did he now?"

"I told him about Joe saying Louie Sam was innocent, too."

Father takes a step toward me. "What's that?"

"Joe said Louie Sam told his mother he didn't murder Mr. Bell."

"And Mr. Osterman told you to keep quiet about that?"

"That's right."

I can see that Father is thrown.

"You're to stay away from Mr. Osterman," he says. "Do you ken me?"

"But I'm working for him, repairing the telegraph line. He's paying a dollar and two bits a day—enough to pay for the doctor, and Teddy's medicine."

Father shakes his head. He's building up steam. When he speaks, his voice is low and dangerous.

"You think I'm not capable of paying for the doctor?"

"No, sir. I mean, yes, sir! I mean …" Nothing is coming out right. "I want to help," I say.

He's quiet for a long moment. He won't look me in the eye. Then he says, "I appreciate that."

He goes out to give Ulysses his feed. Quickly, I pour the milk in my pail into the collecting barrel and follow him outside with a lantern. He's inside the paddock scratching Ulysses's ears while the mule eats from the bag of oats he's holding up for him. Mae noses up to them, wanting her share. He pats her neck, but pushes her away. I know this much about how my Father thinks: rewards must be earned.

"Why don't you like Mr. Osterman?" I ask.

"Who says I don't like him?"

"Father, why don't you?"

There's a long pause. I'm taking a chance pressing the point, but I know that for some reason he is distrustful of Mr. Osterman. Maybe it's the dim evening light that lets him admit that I'm right.

"I heard a story about him," he says. "Seems he spent a goodly amount of time drinking at the Roadhouse when he was younger, before he acquired respectability. One night, he and a mate by the name of John Quin drank corn whiskey 'til they passed out, so Doc Barrow put the two of them in a room to sleep it off. Only problem was, come the morning, Quin wakes up dead."

He gets a wry smile, but I don't see what's funny.

"What killed him?" I ask.

"That's the question, isn't it? Some people say it was the whiskey. But it's curious how people seem to wind up dead around Bill Osterman."

"He's nice to me," I tell him. "Everybody looks up to him."

"You watch yourself around him. That's all I have to say."

Ulysses has finished his oats. Father takes the feed bag into the shed, and I go into the house. Mam is in the rocking chair by the stove with Teddy in her arms. He's sleeping again.

"I told him," I say. "About Mr. Osterman."

"What did he say?"

"To be careful."

"Aye," she says, pulling the blanket up around the baby's head. "That's always good advice."

CHAPTER FOURTEEN

ON FRIDAY AFTERNOON, there's an event that the whole of the Nooksack Valley has been looking forward to for weeks and weeks, before the murder of Mr. Bell took everybody's attention. The governor of the Washington Territory, Dr. William A. Newell himself, is coming to The Crossing all the way from the territorial capitol in Olympia to speak to the issue of statehood, at the behest of Bill Moultray. A dance is to follow in the hall above Mr. Moultray's livery stable, which, truth be told, is the event that most folks have been counting the days toward, at least the younger folks. Before the murder business took hold, all Abigail Stevens and the other girls at school wanted to talk about was their new dresses and hair ribbons.

It's the view of most folks in the Washington Territory that statehood is long overdue. The federal government in that other Washington—the nation's capital—argues back that we don't have enough people in our territory to warrant becoming a state. But along

with the Dakotas and Montana, we keep pushing
for statehood anyway. It's the nature of frontiersmen
to want to rule themselves. We want to elect our
governor, not have him appointed by the president
of the United States, as he is now. And we want
seats in the U.S. Senate, too, instead of our paltry one
seat in the lower house.

Friday at school, Miss Carmichael dismisses us
early so we can all be front row center when the
speeches begin over at The Crossing. By four o'clock, a
lot of folks have turned up in the open space between
Mr. Moultray's store and his livery stable to listen
to the bigwigs. The sun is shining and there's a nice
feeling of excitement in the air, as though everything
is normal again. I scan the crowd for Father, and I feel
happy when I spot him toward the back, talking with
Mr. Stevens, Abigail's father—as though we Gillies,
too, are back to normal.

Dave Harkness is in the crowd, and beside him
stands Mrs. Bell. If she is aware of what people say
about her behind her back, she doesn't seem to care.
She's wearing a fancy hat and holding her chin up
high, as though she wants folks to notice her—
standing beside Mr. Harkness like they belong to
each other, with or without the benefit of a preacher.
I look over to where Pete Harkness is shining up
to a couple of the girls from school. The girls are
giddy at whatever it is he's saying to them, giggling

and carrying on. I wonder what special power the Harkness men have over women. Or maybe it's the women who have the power over them.

Abigail Stevens comes up beside me.

"How do I look, George?" she asks me.

I don't know what to say. She looks pretty, like always, except today she's wearing a bonnet like the grown-up women. Instead of braids, she has dark curls peeking out from under the brim. She bats her eyes.

"You look nice," I tell her.

But that just makes her mad.

"Is that all you got to say?"

I don't know what I said wrong.

"You look very nice."

"For your information," she says, "my mother ordered this hat all the way from Seattle." She lifts the corner of her overcoat to show me the dress she's wearing underneath. "It's to match my new dress for the dance. You're coming to the dance, aren't you?"

"I wasn't planning on it …," I say.

I'm about to impress her with the fact that I can't be up late tonight because I have a job working for Mr. Osterman starting in the morning when she hits me with the little purse she's carrying, which also matches her new dress for the dance.

"You are as slow as a fat toad on a hot day, George Gillies!"

She stomps away. I'm thinking that maybe I should

go after her and find out why she's suddenly acting crazy as a loon, but at that moment several men come out of Moultray's Store, among them Mr. Moultray and Mr. Osterman—and a man I take to be Governor Newell. Chairs have been set up for them along the boardwalk, facing the crowd. Governor Newell is old, tall, and lanky, with big mutton chops. Father says he's a Yankee easterner through and through—the president's man. Father doesn't mean that as flattery.

Mr. Moultray calls for the crowd to quiet down. Like I say, he's a natural leader. When he speaks, people listen.

"Ladies and gentlemen," starts Mr. Moultray. "I thank you for coming out on this fine afternoon to demonstrate to Governor Newell the fervor with which we Washingtonians regard the imminence of statehood."

There's a burst of cheering and applause. Miss Carmichael, who has managed to find a spot directly in front of Mr. Moultray, is clapping so hard she knocks her bonnet crooked.

"It is our hope that Governor Newell will communicate that fervor to the president in Washington, D.C. For it is not a question of if, but *when* the people of this great territory assume their rightful place amongst the republics of the United States of America!"

The crowd is even louder now. Miss Carmichael's

bonnet has flown right off, held on only by the ribbons tied under her chin. Mr. Moultray waits for folks to settle down before continuing at length in the same vein, talking a lot about destiny and God's will. This whole time, Governor Newell is sitting still and stone-faced in his chair. For all I know he's fallen asleep with his eyes open. At last Mr. Moultray finishes speaking, and it's Governor Newell's turn. The governor looks a little startled when Mr. Moultray speaks his name—so maybe he *was* sleeping. He takes his time getting up from his chair.

"Good afternoon," he begins.

The crowd is still, wondering what he'll say next—how, after Mr. Moultray has just finished making such a strong case for statehood, he could have the audacity to tell us we're not yet ready. Before he speaks, he digs into his coat pocket and brings out a folded piece of paper. He opens it up. It appears to be a cable.

"I have here," he says, "a telegraph from Attorney General Davis in Washington, D.C., dated a little over a week ago, on Thursday, the twenty-eighth of February. It pertains to an event that took place at the hands of certain individuals from the Nooksack Valley on the preceding day."

The twenty-eighth is Teddy's birthday. It's also the day after the hanging of Louie Sam. I glance to Mr. Moultray and Mr. Osterman, seated behind the governor. From the way Mr. Osterman's shifting in his chair, it looks like this is one telegraph our telegraph man knows nothing about. And Mr. Moultray looks peaked all of a sudden. It's the same look he wore when Louie Sam told him he was going to fix him. I flash to a memory of Mr. Moultray's hand making contact with that pony's hindquarters. I see bound legs thrashing in midair. My nice normal feeling is chased away.

The governor proceeds to read the telegraph to the crowd.

"'I am requesting in response to a communication from Her Majesty's Government in Canada that you instruct your territorial police to watch out for and arrest members of a lynch mob charged with hanging a Canadian Indian on Canadian soil near Sumas Prairie, British Columbia, pending the Canadians' application for extradition proceedings.'"

The crowd goes dead silent. The governor looks out over the assembled folk of the Nooksack Valley like a judge about to pass sentence.

"Pursuant to these instructions," he says, "I have directed Mr. Bradshaw, the prosecuting attorney of the Third Judicial District in Port Townsend, to act immediately and vigorously against the leaders of this lynch mob so that they can be extradited to Canada, where they will stand trial for their crimes."

Mr. Moultray and Mr. Osterman sit gobsmacked. Or maybe I just think they must be, because I am for sure.

"As to the issue of statehood," says the governor,

"perhaps that is best left to another day."

Having said his piece, Governor Newell stands above us on the boardwalk, as though expecting the leaders of the Nooksack Vigilance Committee to step forward and face judgment this very moment. But nobody moves—except Miss Carmichael, whose hand goes to her mouth as she utters a small cry. I look around to see if Father is still here. He's at the back where he was earlier, standing beside Mr. Stevens. Both of their heads are bowed, eyes hidden by their hat brims. Everybody is silent—until an angry voice booms out of the crowd.

"We was promised a talk on us becoming a state, so let's hear it!"

We all crane our necks to see that the speaker is Dave Harkness. His face is all red with fury. Annette Bell is standing there beside him frowning, with her arms crossed tight. She says something to Mr. Harkness, who then pipes up again.

"If the United States Government has got something to say to us, they can come say it to our faces instead of sending their hired mouthpiece to do it!" he says.

The crowd, so silent a moment ago, sends up a cheer. People are hollering about freedom and democracy, and about how no Washingtonian got to cast a vote to elect Governor Newell to office, so he has no rightful place messing in our business and telling us what to do. Up on the boardwalk, Governor Newell sputters something about how we settlers are ignorant rabble unfit to govern ourselves, which makes the crowd angrier still. Mr. Moultray is on his feet trying to calm everybody down, but he's not trying very hard. When a rock whizzes by the governor, close enough to ruffle his mutton chops, Mr. Moultray whispers something to the men who came with him from Olympia, who then hustle the governor into Moultray's Store. Mr. Moultray turns to the crowd and starts speechifying.

"Fellow citizens of Whatcom County," he says from his perch on the boardwalk. "Surely the Governor can not but help to have comprehended how unwavering is our quest for democracy!"

The crowd sends up another loud cheer. I can't believe how fast the subject has gone from the hanging of Louie Sam back to statehood. I can't believe how the men in the crowd—most of whom rode with the posse that night—don't seem worried about what Governor Newell just said about bringing the leaders to justice. By my count, all five leaders of the posse are present—Mr. Harkness, Mr. Osterman, Mr. Breckenridge, Mr. Hopkins, and Mr. Moultray himself, who at this moment is working folks up into a frenzy of hollering for their rights.

We see no more of the governor. In the crowd, I hear people proclaiming about how Bill Moultray showed the president's man a thing or two. The nerve of him, coming here and reading that telegraph! From the way they talk, it's like the right to statehood has somehow become the same thing as the right to hang Louie Sam, though in my mind they are not the same at all. The first is right and fair. But the hanging ... if folks believe so strongly it was the right thing to do, then why aren't they willing to step up to the governor and tell him so?

AFTER A WHILE, THE CROWD starts to break up. Lots of folks are staying around for the dance later and have brought baskets of food for their dinners. I see Abigail Stevens sitting in a wagon with her parents and her little sisters, eating a sandwich. I think about going over to patch it up with her, to maybe even ask her for a dance if I stay for a little while, but the thought of it makes me break out in a sweat. I head over to Father, who is untethering Ulysses and Mae from a post outside the livery stable. John, Will, and Annie are already seated in the bed of the wagon.

"Are you coming home with us, George?" asks Father.

"He's too busy making eyes at Abigail," says John.

I snarl at him. "Mind your own business, John."

Father gives John a look that makes him hold his tongue.

"Stay if you want to," he says.

I can see Father's holding back from smiling. It's downright humiliating. I climb up into the wagon beside him without saying anything at all, which is enough said. Father slaps Ulysses and Mae with the reins and we start off jostling toward home. After a while, my thoughts stray back to the governor. I ask Father, "Do you think he means what he says about punishing the leaders of the Vigilance Committee?"

Father answers low, so the kids in the back won't hear.

"He can mean it all he wants. What he intends to do about it with the whole valley vowed to secrecy is another question altogether."

"Do you think they ought to be punished?"

Father shoots me a cautioning look. I hold his gaze. I want to know.

"Aye," he says finally. "Aye, I do."

CHAPTER FIFTEEN

I WAKE EARLY SATURDAY MORNING, so I decide to
put the time to good use before I'm due to go see Mr.
Osterman. I'm fishing for trout in the creek at a good
spot I know upstream from the mill. It's chilly this
early, but the sun is shining and you can feel spring
just around the corner. After a few minutes I feel a big
tug on my line. I see a brown back fin crest before the
fish swims back down into the water, taking my line
with him. He's big, maybe a five-pounder. I give him
his head for a bit, then slowly I reel him in, feeling
for just the right amount of tension to keep him on
the hook. When he gets close to the shore, he gets an
inkling that he's being played and makes a run for it. I
know that's my do-or-die moment, so I give the line a
big yank—and pull the trout right up onto the shore.
He's flopping around in the grass like a demon before
I take a rock and end it for him.

"He's a beaut!"

I spin around, taken by surprise. Who should be
sauntering along a deer path but Joe Hampton. He's

got a fishing pole with him that must have belonged to his pa—the Indians usually use traps and spears to fish.

"Mind if I join you?" he says.

I am not in a position to say no—neither of our families claims this stretch of the creek, and in fact we are closer to his shack than to our cabin.

"Suit yourself," I say.

He digs in the bank for a worm, which he hooks and then casts into the water. We sit in the grass twenty feet from each other, tugging at our lines, listening to birds sing. I am dying for him to tell me about what happened with his *tillicums* across the border. He stays quiet, making me speak first.

"When did you get back?"

"Couple of days ago."

He falls back into silence. I see he means to make me work for crumbs of information. I decide to surprise him with some of my own.

"I hear the Canadian Government has been calming your people down."

"If you mean they sent an Indian agent in, that's true. Patrick McTiernan. But he came because the Stó:lō asked him to come."

I don't like his attitude, like he's always got the upper hand.

"So are they attacking or not?" I challenge him.

"We thought about it. There was something like

two hundred people there. We talked all day and all night about what should be done. Some people thought we should come across the border and hang the first sixty-five Americans we came across, that that would be a nice round number to even the score for an innocent boy hanged. But most people thought it would be enough to take the first white man we found, carry him back to the hanging tree where Louie Sam died and string him up. An eye for an eye."

At that moment I get another bite on my line. I pull it up. It's only a catfish, but I'm glad that the business of landing it gives me a reason to turn my face away from Joe, because the picture of two hundred angry Indians coming over the border to hang sixty-five of us, or even one of us, is giving me the willies. I keep my back to Joe as I crouch down to unhook the fish.

"So what did the Indian agent say to that?"

"He wasn't big on that idea," says Joe. "He wanted us to think twice about starting a feud that could wind up in a full-fledged war. Even though it's plain as the nose on your face that we didn't start it."

"So how was it left then?"

"There was one thing that everybody could agree on. There has to be an investigation, to figure out who really killed Jim Bell."

Words start in my mouth to deny Louie Sam's innocence, but I say nothing. Joe Hampton gives me a satisfied look, like I've just admitted that Louie Sam is not the culprit.

"The chiefs agreed not to bring a raiding party across the border. They sent the people back to their home villages. They're leaving it up to the Canadian law to find the murderers."

"Murderers. You think more than one person killed Mr. Bell?" I ask.

He looks at me like I'm some kind of idiot.

"I'm talking about the murderers of Louie Sam," he says. "If it was up to me, every last murdering son of a bitch that rode with that lynch mob would pay for what they done."

He keeps looking at me, as if to say that he knows that I'm one of them. I turn away and throw the catfish back into the creek. I watch it swim down into the muddy depths, all the while feeling Joe Hampton's eyes hooking into me. A *murderer*. Is that what he's saying I am?

I CARRY THE TROUT HOME so Mam can fry it for the noon meal. All the while I'm walking, I'm thinking. I want to believe that Louie Sam murdered James Bell. I want to believe it, but I have so many questions. I keep seeing him in my mind, at the moment when Mr. Moultray put the rope around his neck. I see the expression on his face—scared to death, but angry, too. If he was guilty, he would have acted guilty. Wouldn't he? I keep thinking about the fact that Louie Sam was wearing a pair of suspenders when they hauled him out of Mr. York's farmhouse. I wish I knew what happened to the suspenders we found in the swamp. I would like to see for myself whether they're man-sized or boy-sized. If they were man-sized, then it would have to follow that maybe it wasn't Louie Sam running away through the swamp. But who was it then? And whoever it was, was that the person who shot Mr. Bell?

WHEN I REACH THE cabin, I give the trout to John to clean. He complains about it, but I have to be on my way into Nooksack to meet Mr. Osterman at the appointed time. For myself, I take bread and two boiled eggs to eat as I walk. I am not about to ask Father if I can take Mae. Since I told him about my job repairing telegraph poles, he has said nothing more to me about it. Mam is pleased there will be a little more money, but she's worried about what kind of work I'll be doing, and how dangerous it will be. I'm wondering about that, too. But Teddy's medicine is almost used up. If Mr. Osterman gives me a day's wages today, I will have more than enough to settle Mam's account with Dr. Thompson for the last bottle, as well as to purchase a new one to bring home with me.

When I reach the Nooksack Hotel, the door to the telegraph office is open, but Mr. Osterman is not at his desk. I knock on the door, thinking that maybe he's in there, but hidden from my view. There's no answer. I am unsure what to do, whether to go in and wait for him, or to stand out here in the lobby of the hotel. I look across to Mr. Hopkins, thinking to ask him if he knows Mr. Osterman's whereabouts, but he is busy looking after a red-headed man whom I guess to be a hotel guest. I look from that man's mud-caked boots to his worn buckskin coat and I wonder how he has the money to stay in such a fancy place. Now Mr. Hopkins is peering at me over his spectacles, looking me up and down in my fish-stinking dungarees and jacket, like between me and the red-haired man, he's had enough of varmints like us dirtying up his nice hotel. I'm expecting him to tell me any minute now to go wait outside.

"I've got business with Mr. Osterman," I tell him.

"What business have you got?"

"He hired me," I say, and add for emphasis just in case I haven't made my point, "I'm working for him."

The red-headed man turns around and gives me a look. He throws me a friendly smile, then picks up his beaten-up valise and starts climbing the spiral staircase to the rooms upstairs.

"Go wait in the telegraph office," Mr. Hopkins tells me.

I decide that must be what Mr. Osterman intended for me to do all along.

A QUARTER OF AN HOUR goes by. I'm getting the fidgets just standing in the middle of the room waiting. There's a fine leather chair beside the fireplace, but I don't feel right sitting in it in my smelly work clothes. The oak desk chair, on the other hand, has a cushion I could remove. Also, it's a swivel chair. I have never in my life sat in a swivel chair.

I peek outside into the hotel lobby to see if there is any sign of Mr. Osterman. There is none. I lean across the desk and look out the window into the street. It's silent as the grave out there. So I remove the cushion from the swivel chair and I sit down. I swing myself a little to the left, then a little to the right, imagining what it must be like to be the telegraph man. I place my finger on the small black key that Mr. Osterman uses to send messages. I'm tempted to give a tap or two, but I worry that I might wind up sending a message to some other telegraph man down the line.

I don't mean to stick my nose into telegraph office business, but there in front of me among the papers on the desk I can't help but see a newspaper, and in that newspaper a headline leaps out at me—"The Sumas Tragedy." The newspaper is the *British Columbian*, published across the border in the town of New Westminster. The story is all about the hanging of Louie Sam, and the meeting of the Canadian Indians at Sumas that Joe Hampton went to. I can't believe

I'm reading about us in the newspaper, like we're as famous as Wild Bill Hickok!

Deploring the lynching of fourteen-year-old Louie Sam as an illegal act, Indian agent Patrick McTiernan promised local chiefs that the Dominion Government will do everything in its power to bring those who are responsible to justice.

British Columbia Premier William Smithe has sent an appeal to Prime Minister Sir John A. Macdonald in Ottawa, who has demanded that officials in Washington D.C. and in the Washington Territory identify the leaders of the American lynch mob.

"Out of my chair!"

Mr. Osterman is standing in the doorway, red-faced with anger. I leap up so fast I almost make the swivel chair fall over.

"Mr. Hopkins said to wait in here …," I stammer like a fool.

"That means wait, not snoop."

Mr. Osterman crosses to his desk. He sees what I was reading, snatches up the newspaper. He's glaring at me. All I can think to say is, "He was only fourteen."

"You never mind how old anybody was."

"Are we in trouble with the law?"

"Just keep your mouth shut and everything's going to be fine."

"But the Canadians—"

"To hell with the damned Canadians!"

Mr. Osterman yells so loud that the whole hotel must be able to hear him, even the guests upstairs. I remember what my father said about him finding respectability only lately, like he wasn't always respectable. I wonder if I'm catching a glimpse of his previous self. But he calms down a bit, maybe because he's worried other people might hear.

"I am sick and tired of people sticking their noses where they don't belong—and that includes you."

"I'm sorry, Mr. Osterman."

"Did I make a mistake offering you this job, George?"

That makes me panic.

"No, sir!" I tell him.

"Can I rely on your discretion?" I'm not sure what he means by that. It must show, because then he says, "Can I count on you to do what's right, to be a loyal citizen of Nooksack?"

"Yes, sir. No question."

He eyes me a moment longer, like he's making up his mind about me.

"All right, then. You just do as you're told, and we'll get along fine."

"Yes, sir," I say.

I'm so relieved, I want to cry—but I keep my face calm, to show him he can trust me to keep my word. He turns to a shelf of books and takes down a scroll, which when he spreads it out on the desk turns out to be a map of the telegraph line. He jabs his finger at the section of line that runs from the far side of the Nooksack River—the part that runs west and south toward Ferndale.

"I want you to start here and work your way west. Mr. Harkness will let you ride the ferry across the river for free."

I don't stop to think before I ask, "But what about the stretch around Mr. Bell's cabin?"

He brings the flat of his hand down hard on the desk. "Did you or did you not just promise me to do as you're told!"

"I did! I'm sorry! I will!"

I'm kicking myself like crazy. Why can't I learn to keep my big mouth shut? He rolls up the map, his face a fury. I'm sure he's about to tell me I'm fired before I even begin. But after a minute, he says, "Does your pa own a handsaw you can use?"

"Yes, sir."

I'm thinking that asking Father to allow me to take it will be a hazard, but I am on such thin ice with Mr. Osterman that I am not about to tell him "no."

"Good. Your job is to cut back the underbrush

growing up around the poles, to keep it away from the wire."

"Yes, sir."

"You check the pole for rot, top to bottom, and for damage from insects and birds. Mr. Moultray will supply you with pitch for patching. Tell him to put it on my account."

"Yes, sir."

I want to know how I'm supposed to climb up the poles, but I'm afraid to ask in case I look dumb.

"A day's work is dawn to dusk. Get an early start tomorrow. You can come by here for your wages on Monday."

So I won't be paid today, not even tomorrow— never mind that tomorrow is Sunday and I'll have to miss church again. But I am in no position to complain about working on the Sabbath, nor to ask Mr. Osterman for the money in advance.

"Yes, sir," I say. "Thank you, sir."

I LEAVE THE HOTEL DOWN-HEARTED and cross the street to Dr. Thompson's drug store. Mrs. Thompson is behind the counter, talking with a customer. The customer is Mrs. Stevens, Abigail's mother. They greet me with smiles. It makes me happy that not all of Nooksack is against us Gillies.

"How's the new baby?" Mrs. Thompson asks me.

"Still sickly."

Mrs. Thompson looks worried for us. So does Mrs. Stevens.

"Winter babies have a hard time of it," she says, "even if the winter is mild."

"I'll be with you in just a moment," Mrs. Thompson tells me kindly.

She goes back to wrapping Mrs. Stevens's purchases, continuing the conversation they were having when I came in.

"I heard he was planning to sue, for estrangement of affection," says Mrs. Thompson.

Mrs. Stevens raises her eyebrows and clucks her tongue.

"What do these men see in that woman?" she says.

"A lonely man is easily misled," pronounces Mrs. Thompson.

"How far misled is the question," says Mrs. Stevens.

Mrs. Thompson drops her voice to a whisper.

"I can't believe he would go that far."

Mrs. Stevens shakes her head sadly.

"Susannah must be turning over in her grave," she replies.

I know who they're talking about. Susannah must be Susannah Harkness, Pete Harkness's ma, who died three years back. And "that woman" can be no other than Mrs. Bell.

Mrs. Stevens says good-bye to Mrs. Thompson and leaves the store, telling me to give her regards to Mam.

"Now then," says Mrs. Thompson to me, "it was the fever tonic Dr. Thompson ordered for the little one, wasn't it? That's seventy-five cents."

She turns and takes a bottle of it from the shelf behind her and sets it on the counter. She's waiting for her money. I'm standing there with my tongue tied.

"Could I pay you on Monday, ma'am? For both bottles?"

She's frowning a little now. I'm afraid that we Gillies have reached the end of her charity.

"That's two bottles on your account. Are you sure you'll have the money then, George?"

"Yes, ma'am! I've got a job, working for Mr. Osterman."

She gives me a queer look.

"And what might you be doing for Mr. Osterman?"

"Repairing poles."

"Do your parents know about this?"

"Yes, ma'am."

"And they approve?"

"Yes, ma'am."

She smiles, but her smile is tighter than before. She pushes the bottle toward me.

"All right, then, George. I'll see you on Monday."

Mam is so grateful to me for bringing the medicine that she gives me a slice of apple pie when I get home. She isn't happy about me spending all day Sunday away from home missing church and all, but she says that sacrifices must be made. She's only sorry that it's my immortal soul that's doing the sacrificing. It's quiet in the house for once. John and Will are out in the fields with Father, and Annie has Isabel in the yard teaching her to dance—though she herself doesn't know a waltz from a two-step. Teddy is awake in his cradle by the stove, but he's not crying or fussing. He's just lying there. Mam gets her mending basket and sits at the table with me while I eat.

"Mam, what's 'estrangement of affection'?" I ask.

"Why would you want to know such a thing?" she asks me back.

"I heard Mrs. Thompson say it. She was talking about Mr. Harkness, and Mrs. Bell."

I see in Mam's face that a penny has dropped.

"Was she?" she says.

Suddenly, she's concentrating hard on the hole in the sock she has stretched over her hand.

"Tell me," I say. "What does it mean?"

She stays quiet.

"Mam, I'm fifteen. I need to know about the world."

Now she looks up at me. She has a sad smile.

"Aye, so you do," she says. Then, "'Estrangement of affection' is when somebody comes between a man and a woman who are married, or engaged to be married."

"And you can be sued for that?"

"Aye, you can."

Now I'm starting to understand.

"So … Mr. Bell wanted to sue Mr. Harkness, for coming between him and Mrs. Bell?"

Mam's interest perks up.

"Is that what Mrs. Thompson said?"

"I'm pretty sure that's who she was talking about."

"Well, then … yes. I suppose that in Mr. Bell's mind he had cause to sue Mr. Harkness."

I dig my fork into the pie and swallow another bite. We sit together in silence for a bit, Mam sewing, and me thinking that I never knew before there were such bad feelings between Mr. Bell and Mr. Harkness. But then, how could there not have been?

CHAPTER SIXTEEN

JOHN IS DOING THE MILKING Sunday morning when I come into the shed. I take Father's handsaw down from its nail. John is watching me while he milks.

"Did you ask him if you can take that?" he wants to know.

"Why don't you mind your own business, John?" I say, because the truth is I didn't ask Father. I'm hoping I can return the saw before he notices it's missing. I put it in a knapsack with the bread and cheese that Mam has given me, and set out along the track toward The Crossing with the sun barely peeking over the trees.

This is the second Sunday since Mr. Bell died. By the time I reach the remains of his cabin, the sun is high enough to send sparkles off the frosty rime that's spread over the charred timbers like white moss. It's almost pretty. I haven't had breakfast yet, so I stop and eat some of the bread and cheese. While I chew I walk the length of the ruins. Kids have started talking at school about this stretch of the track being haunted by Mr. Bell's ghost, but the place doesn't feel haunted to me. It just feels lonely. It always felt lonely, though, even when Mr. Bell was alive.

I come to the spot between what used to be his store and his kitchen—the spot where we found his body—and I wonder what it was about him that made his wife and son hate him so. But did she hate him enough to want him dead? Is that what Mrs. Thompson and Mrs. Stevens were driving at? It doesn't seem possible that we have a murderer living right here in our midst. But if it's true that Louie Sam didn't kill Mr. Bell, then somebody else must have done it. I set out walking again. My mind is full of such thoughts all the way to The Crossing—about Mr. Bell hating Mr. Harkness for stealing his wife away, and Mrs. Bell hating her husband all the more for the trouble he was causing her and Mr. Harkness. I just don't know what to believe.

When I reach Mr. Moultray's store, it's closed. In the livery stable I find Jack Simpson, the man the posse sent ahead to sneak into Mr. York's farmhouse. He tells me to give him a minute and he'll get the pitch I need for the repairs from the supplies shed. I watch him feed and water the last of the horses. Jack's a friendly type with a quick smile, though he smells bad from having no mother or wife to wash his clothes or tell him to take a bath. He's close enough to my age that I feel like I can ask him a question.

"What do you make of Governor Newell saying

he's going to track down the leaders of the Vigilance Committee?" I say.

"He can try," he replies with a laugh.

"Mr. York saw your face. He knows who you are."

"Mr. York is a good actor," says Jack.

"What do you mean?"

"The way he was huffin' and puffin' at the posse, that was all for show. He knew we was coming for the Indian."

"Who told him?"

"Never you mind," says Jack.

He gives me a warning look and goes silent— which is unusual for Jack, who's a big talker by nature. I follow him out of the livery to a shed, where he opens a barrel and starts ladling gooey black pitch into a bucket for me. I've got one more question I'm itching to ask.

"What was he like?"

"Who?"

"Louie Sam. You saw him that night, didn't you? Inside the farmhouse."

"I didn't see him. They had him in a back room." Then he adds, not being one to miss a chance to puff himself up, "Mr. York told me about him, though."

"What did he say?"

"That he was quiet. That he came with Sheriff Leckie and Mr. Campbell peaceable enough when they arrested him."

"Joe Hampton says Louie Sam told his mother he didn't do it."

Jack halts what he's doing, pitch dripping from the ladle. He gets hot under the collar.

"Who cares what Joe Hampton says?"

"But what if it's the truth? What if we got the wrong fella?"

Jack spits into the straw. "It don't matter. I would kill a Chinaman as quick as I would an Indian," he says. "And I would kill an Indian as quick as I would a dog."

Jack Simpson has a reputation for being likable, but at this moment I don't see why. He seems all bluster and hate to me.

"He was only fourteen," I tell him.

Jack's face goes all dark and he stabs his finger at me.

"You Gillies ought to remember who your friends are," he says. "Just keep your trap shut."

He shoves the bucket of pitch at me and walks away without so much as a "so long."

I've done it again—opened my mouth when I shouldn't have. Still, I'm sick and tired of people telling me to keep quiet.

I HEAD DOWN THE HILL from the livery to the ferry landing. The ferry is a scow that's tethered to a heavy rope that's been strung from one shore of the Nooksack River to the other. The river is shallow here and calm compared to where it comes rollicking down from Mount Baker to the south and east of us. Unless you have your own boat or barge, the ferry is the only way to cross if you want to travel to Ferndale or Bellingham. It costs twenty-five cents for a person to cross, and fifty cents for a horse, or any other animal with four legs instead of two.

There's nobody around when I reach the ferry. The scow is moored at the short dock, its belly pooled with water from last night's rain. In part I'm relieved not to have to face Mr. Harkness, considering the thoughts I've been having about him. But by rights I should be across the river by now inspecting telegraph poles. So I walk up the path to the house where Pete lives with his pa and Mrs. Bell and Jimmy. Mr. Bell's horse is in a small paddock. He ambles over when he sees me coming and sticks his neck out over the split rails. Maybe he recollects me from the night Pete and I rode him north. More likely he's hungry and wondering if I have something for him to eat.

I'm remembering the times I used to come here to see Pete on a summer day, how Mrs. Harkness—Pete's real mother—would give us hotcakes left over from breakfast, with jam. Then we'd go fish in the river, or set snares for rabbits in the woods. We could spend hours at one adventure or another. The house doesn't look much different from when Mrs. Harkness lived here. It doesn't look like a den of iniquity. There's smoke coming from the chimney, so I know folks are up and about inside. I walk up and knock on the door. Nothing happens, so I knock harder.

Jimmy Bell opens the door. His eyes still show signs of bruising, traces of the beating he took from John a week ago.

"What do you want?" he says, not at all pleased to see me standing there. I suppose that one Gillies is as bad as another to him.

"I need to get across the river," I reply. "I'm repairing poles for Mr. Osterman."

As proof, I hold up my bucket of pitch.

"Pa!" he yells into the house.

I'm thinking, isn't that interesting, that he calls Mr. Harkness his pa?

"What is it?" comes a holler from inside.

"George Gillies says he needs to get across the river!"

In another second, the door swings wider. But it isn't Mr. Harkness who's standing beside Jimmy. It's Pete. He looks me up and down like I'm some kind of trash that's landed on his stoop.

"What do you need to cross the river for, George? There some Indians over there you want to go pow-wow with?"

There he goes again, calling me an Indian lover. When did Pete develop this mean streak?

"For your information," I tell him, "I've got work to

do over there for your uncle."

"You got twenty-five cents?" he asks.

"Mr. Osterman says I don't have to pay," I reply.

Mr. Harkness arrives at the door just as I'm telling Pete this. He's pulling up his suspenders and his dark hair is wild, like he just got out of bed. He seems even taller framed by a door meant for normal-sized people.

"He does, does he?" says Mr. Harkness. Between his size and his growl, he makes me think of a big black bear. To be honest, Mr. Harkness has always frightened me a little.

"He says he's repairing telegraph poles," Jimmy pipes up.

Mr. Harkness looks at my bucket of pitch, then he looks at me. He lets out a hard laugh. "You take him," he says to Pete. Then, to me, "Go wait down by the ferry."

He slams the door in my face.

I WAIT A GOOD QUARTER of an hour at the ferry before Pete comes sauntering down the path. He tells me to climb into the scow, while he unties the moorings. My boots are sitting in two inches of water in the bottom of the ferry. I look at the river. Even though it's pretty shallow here, the water's cold and the current is fast-moving. I wonder where Mr. Hampton drowned, whether it was near to this shore or the other, or in the middle. It's a famous story around here. The ferry was just a canoe then. It was late spring and the water was high. Mr. Hampton set out to fetch a traveler from the other side when a log struck the canoe and split it in half. They say his family was watching from the shore when he was thrown into the raging current. I wonder if Joe watched his pa drown.

"Have you done this before?" I ask.

"'Course I have," Pete snaps.

He jumps into the scow and hands me a pail.

"Start bailing," he says, picking up the long pole he'll use to push us across.

"That's your job," I tell him.

"My job is to push your lazy butt across this river," he says. "Anyway, you're riding for free, so don't act like I'm your hired hand or something."

Pete sinks the pole into the water and gives a shove, throwing his whole body into it. As the scow shifts away from the dock, I can feel the current pushing at the boat, trying to send it downstream. The water at my feet is sloshing around. I fill the pail and start bailing over the side.

"How much is Uncle Bill paying you?" Pete asks.

"A dollar and half a day."

"What?!" I'm pleased by his jealousy. "Why the hell would he hire you, anyway? I'd do it for a dollar, and I'm his kin."

"Guess he figures he can rely on me," I say.

"Are you trying to say I'm not reliable?"

"Pete, if you want to know why he hired me instead of you, go ask him yourself."

That shuts him up. We're nearing the middle of the river now. The scow is straining against the cable. It's taking all of Pete's muscle power to keep it moving forward. If he hadn't been acting so high and mighty lately, I'd go and help him.

"I see Mrs. Bell has claimed that horse for herself," I say.

"That's none of your business."

"I just wonder what Mr. Bell would think about that."

"Mr. Bell ain't in a condition to do much thinking."

"Did she get the gold, too?"

"What gold?"

"Five hundred dollars of it. Mr. Moultray found it in Mr. Bell's cabin, after it burned."

"I don't know anything about that."

"If Mrs. Bell stood to get the gold as well as the horse, doesn't it seem like she would have liked to have seen Mr. Bell dead?"

"What foolishness are you talking now? You think she got that Indian to go commit murder for her?"

But I can see that Pete's thinking it over, that the idea that his more-or-less stepmother was involved has never dawned on him before this moment.

I say, "You tell me. You're the one who saw Louie Sam that day."

"Damn right, I did!" he barks.

"Aren't you going to tell me how he had murder in his eyes?"

That makes him so angry, he stops poling.

"I know what I saw!" he cries.

For a moment I think I've gone too far—that he might dump me over the side of the scow into the river. But there's confusion in his face as well as anger.

"Cool off," I tell him. "You're awful touchy about it."

"Shut your mouth or I'll shut it for you," says Pete, pushing the pole again—refusing to so much as look at me.

As we reach the shore, Pete tries to slow the scow down, but we're coming in too fast. We plough into the dock with a jolt, gouging the boards.

"Your pa won't like that," I say.

I climb out of the scow and tell Pete—who's still not talking to me—to watch for my return in the afternoon. I head on down the telegraph trail without looking back, happy that for once I've had the last word.

CHAPTER SEVENTEEN

THE FIRST TELEGRAPH POLE I come to is a thirty-footer just a few paces from the water. The telegraph cable stretches up from where it was laid across the riverbed. The underwater part of the wire is coated in rubber, but where it meets the glass insulator at the top of the pole that's there to support it, the wire is bare copper. This pole is out in the open, so there's not much brush around it to speak of. Truth be told, I'm not altogether clear on what I'm supposed to be looking for. The wire looks to my eye like it's sitting well on the insulator, and the pole looks free from damage from birds or bugs. So I walk on.

In seconds, the telegraph wire carries messages that used to take days or weeks to get through by stagecoach or train. The line runs pole to pole over mountains and over gorges. It took hundreds of men years and years to string the wire, through some of the wildest country you are ever likely to find. But I have a nice flat trail to follow—though the forest is thick and wild on either side.

The next pole is a hundred feet along the trail. The line looks good on this one, too, from what I can see from the ground, but the ground is swampy here and brambles have been taking full advantage of that fact, sending long sprouting branches up. I take out the handsaw and cut off a few. Then I think I may as well clear out the whole bush. It has thorns that catch at my hands and jacket. It takes me a good while before I'm finished. Once I have the brush cleared away from the pole, I can see a soft spot in the wood, so I find a suitable length of branch in the woods and use it to layer on some pitch.

I tuck the handsaw in my belt and walk on from pole to pole, hacking away brush where needed. Once or twice I have to shimmy up the pole a little ways to apply some pitch. I collect several sticks of various lengths for this purpose.

By late morning the sky has clouded up. There could be more rain. I'm heading to my twenty-third pole when I see coming toward me a family of Indians. This makes me nervous, me being the only white person in who knows how many miles. There's no way of telling whether these Indians are friendly or not, and I'm wishing I'd brought more than a handsaw with me. A hatchet would have been a comfort, or a rifle. But we only have the one rifle, which is for Father's use—although I'm allowed to use it for shooting rabbits and the like.

I keep one eye on the telegraph line, and one on the Indians. As we draw closer to each other, I see that it's just two women and a bunch of kids, so I relax a bit. But they're staring at me, which makes me uncomfortable. One of them is not much older than Abigail Stevens. She says something to the older one, her mam I presume, in their gibberish, and they both start laughing. From the way they keep staring, they can only be laughing at me. Now the kids start in giggling. I had not intended to talk to them, but now I can't help myself.

"What's so funny?" I say.

We're all stopped in the middle of the trail. One of the little kids, a boy about Isabel's size, starts prancing around, holding his hands up to the side of his head like the devil's horns. I figure it's some kind of heathen dance. Whatever it is he's doing, the Indians think he's pure hilarity, because now they're clutching their middles they're laughing so hard. That just makes the boy dance harder. He's loving the attention his antics are getting from the women.

But it seems his big sister, a girl of Annie's age, isn't amused by him. She grabs him hard by both arms and tries to make him stop, just the way Annie likes to boss Isabel. The boy's face crumples and he builds into an ear-splitting wail. Now the mother is in the middle of it, pulling the two kids apart, scolding her daughter, comforting the boy. I don't need to understand their language to get the gist of what she's saying. I know what *my* mam would be saying.

Nobody's laughing as they walk on. The mother, the girl, and the little boy are all cross-tempered. But the other woman, the young one, turns back.

"Man," she says, meaning me. She points to her head, and then to mine. *"Mowitsh."*

I feel my hair, and discover that I've got twigs stuck on either side of my head from clearing brush. So that's what the boy was making fun of. I nod, to let her know I understand. She smiles back, shy-like, then she catches up to the rest of them.

"Thank you!" I call after her.

She turns back and smiles again.

THERE'S A POLE EVERY two hundred feet or so along the trail, roughly twenty-five to a mile. By my fiftieth pole, I've covered about two miles. It's well past noon when I stop for a break. I sit on a stump, damp though it is on my behind, and take out the bread and cheese Mam sent with me. The day isn't warm, but the work has given me a thirst. I wish I had some water, but there's no stream nearby. As much as I'm tired and could stand to rest a little longer, I'm mindful that I want to make a good impression on Mr. Osterman, this being my first day on the job. I put what remains of my food in the knapsack for later, tuck the saw in my belt, pick up my pitch bucket and sticks, and keep moving.

When I get past the fiftieth pole, I see I have a problem with the fifty-first. Something has knocked the telegraph wire off of the glass insulator. It's hanging down in a big loop between poles fifty and fifty-two, ten feet off the ground. How am I meant to climb the pole way up to the top to put the wire back in place? I need a ladder, but there's none for miles around. I see, though, how a nearby cedar tree is growing at an angle toward the pole. If I climb the tree and use my longest pitch stick, maybe I can reach the wire and lift it back onto the insulator.

I'm jumping to pull myself up onto the bottom branch of the cedar when suddenly it's like I hear Mam speaking to me. "Be careful, George," she's saying. I remember the handsaw I have stuck through my belt. I take it out and lay it safely on the ground beside the knapsack and the pitch bucket. Then I start climbing with my longest pitch stick tucked under my arm. The main branches of the cedar are nice and wide, but there are lots of little branches that block my way. I think about climbing down for the handsaw. But I reach a branch that is roughly on the same level as the dangling line and fight my way through the cedar leaves until I find an open patch.

I'm in luck—the telegraph wire is in view, just a few feet out from the branch. When I stretch my arm I can just touch the wire with my pitch stick. But all I'm doing is making it swing away from me. I need to hook it somehow, so I climb farther up to the height of the insulator so I can catch the wire from underneath and put it back where it belongs.

The branch is wide enough for me to stand up on. Once I'm standing, I slide my boots along the surface toward the wire, grabbing at other branches to keep my balance. The branch is getting thinner, but it's still holding my weight all right. Finally, I reckon I am close enough. I reach my pitch stick under the wire and give it a good tap to make it swing toward me. The first time, it's still outside my reach. But the second time I've got it. I reach out and grab the wire.

The wire burns into the palm of my hand like the vibrating sting of a giant bee. The shock of it pulses up my arm. I'm so surprised I don't even think about the sensible thing to do, which would be to let go of the wire. I stand there like a fool holding on. I'm feeling light-headed. I'm losing my footing. Everything is going black. The last thing I remember is I'm falling through the branches, being scratched and bumped. I do not remember hitting the ground.

WHEN I WAKE UP, my first thought is how quiet it is. I wonder why there's no sound of my brothers and sisters chattering to each other, or of Mam at the stove fixing breakfast. Slowly it comes to me where I am, and what happened.

I'm lying on my back under pole number fifty-one.

Judging by the gloom collecting among the trees along the trail, it's late in the afternoon. My throat is parched. I look at my right hand, the one I used to grab the wire. It's burned and blistered. But it's my left arm that's throbbing with pain. It's pinned under my back at a peculiar angle. Propping myself on my right elbow, I try to sit up—but the pain from my other arm shoots up into my neck and makes me cry out. I lie on my back, thinking what to do. It's so still you could hear a twig snap from a mile away, but I don't even hear that.

"Hello?" I call, hoping that by some miracle somebody might be near enough to help me—maybe that Indian family I met earlier, making their way home from wherever they had been. Those women would know what to do for my arm, how to make a splint for it and wrap it tight. "Hello!?"

But there's no one. I look up at the telegraph wire, just visible in the growing darkness, still hanging in a loop the way I found it. *So that's what electricity feels like*, I think to myself—a detail Mr. Osterman neglected to tell me. I think: *If I had pulled the line down with me and broken it, the telegraph messages couldn't get through and at least he would know something was wrong.* But the telegraph line is fine. I'm the one that is broken.

I know I can't stay here. The forest is quiet now, but cougars hunt by night, and wolves and bears are always on the prowl. I take a few deep breaths and push myself up so that I'm sitting. The pain from my left arm shoots up and down my body, but I tell myself that if I just hold still it will steady—and it does a little. I take a few more deep breaths, and I push myself up to my feet. I think I'm going to pass out from the pain. Somehow my foggy brain wills my feet to move, one in front of the other, up the trail the way I came—toward The Crossing. I have two whole miles to go and I have to get there before the Harknesses shut down the ferry for the night.

Every step sends a new tremor through me until even my teeth ache. I discover that if I use my burned right hand to hold my left elbow tight against my body while I walk, the pain subsides a little. After a while I cheer up, which is strange. Truth be told, I feel a bit the way I felt when Pete Harkness and I helped ourselves to his pa's jug of Doc Barrow's liquor. Light-headed in a pleasant way. A little silly.

I start slowing my pace. I tell myself to stop worrying so much about getting to The Crossing. All I really want to do is sleep. I feel like I practically *am* sleeping, though I'm walking, too. I start thinking that it wouldn't matter if I lay down right here and closed my eyes, just for a little while. Then I stumble on a tree root, and the pain from my arm and shoulder rips through me—waking me. I know I have to keep walking, before the sleepiness overtakes me again.

Suddenly, I'm aware of something moving through the woods beside the trail, following alongside me. Whatever it is, it's light-footed—flitting between the trees like no more than a shadow. The funny thing is, I don't feel afraid. Whatever it is, I don't think it means me harm. Maybe this is what the preachers mean about walking with God. But then I see that whoever it is, he's human, not animal—not God. He's small—a kid, like me.

"Who's there?" I say. He doesn't answer. I lose sight of him when a clump of bushes comes between us and I panic a little, because seeing him makes me feel less lonesome. I'm relieved he's still there when we reach the other side of the bushes, his legs keeping pace with mine.

"Who are you?" Still no answer. "Show yourself!"

And then, ahead of me, he steps out of the woods. He's facing me on the trail, blocking my way. I stop walking. The light is so dim now that I can't make out his features. But I know who he is. I know him from his broad face and his defiant look, the way he holds his chin up and throws his shoulders back.

"Are you a ghost?" I say.

He still won't answer. He's just standing there, like a statue. I step closer. I see his eyes now, dark coals burning into me. But there's light in them, too, like he's just heard a good joke. His face is soft and full, like a little kid's face. Like the dancing boy's face.

Why isn't he angry? He should be angry!

"I'm sorry," I tell him. "I'm sorry I didn't speak up—about the suspenders. I'm sorry for leaving you there in that clearing, all alone." Now I'm choking up. I'm crying. "I'm sorry for your mam!"

At last he speaks.

"George Gillies," he says, "what the hell are you babbling about?"

I'm confused. I look again. A moment ago I could have sworn it was Louie Sam standing there, but instead it's Pete Harkness.

"I've been waiting for you for hours," he says. He holds up a lantern as he steps closer, showing alarm at the sight of me. "George? What happened to you?"

I'm about ready to pass out.

"I'm sorry," I say.

They seem the only words I'm capable of just now.

Chapter Eighteen

Pete half carries, half drags me the rest of the way along the trail to the river, lighting our way with the lantern. The breeze has picked up. By the time we reach the ferry, wind is pushing the clouds away from the moon, which is full and bright. Pete helps me into the scow. I'm shivering, so he finds some old gunnysacks to lie on top of me to keep me warm. He pushes off from the shore. That's when I remember,

"The handsaw!"

"What handsaw?"

"My father's. I left it. I have to go back."

I struggle to get up on my feet.

"Stay put!" shouts Pete. He's working up a good speed, pushing hard on the pole. "You're in no shape to be hiking that trail in the dark."

"He'll have my hide," I say.

"My pa will have my ass for running the ferry so late!"

"Why are you?"

"Because you said you were coming back, and you

didn't show up."

It's taken me this long to realize that Pete could have left me on the far shore for the night, but instead he came looking for me down the trail. I'm still too put off with him to muster a thank you. Instead I say, "I have to get that saw."

"I'll go look for it in the morning."

"You've got school in the morning."

"So I'll skip school," he says, like I'm being dumb.

I lie back on some coils of rope on the floor of the scow. My need to sleep is taking over again.

"Your pa will be too glad to see you alive to tan you," Pete says, by way of easing my worry. I'm glad to see a glimmer of the old Pete, my friend. "Do your folks know where you are?"

"They knew where I was going, but I was supposed to be back tonight."

"You'll have to stay with us tonight. You can go home in the morning, if you're up to it. Otherwise, I'll get word to them."

"Why are you doing this?" I say.

"Doing what?"

"Being nice."

"You think you got the corner on being good, George?"

"I never said that."

"That's how you act. Like you're better than me. That's how all you Gillies act. Superior."

171

Well that takes all. I'm thinking of the night that Louie Sam died, when Pete and his pa were behaving like the biggest toads in the puddle, telling everybody what to do. Humiliating my father in front of the whole town.

"Seems to me you've got that the wrong way round, Pete."

"How do you figure that?"

"You're the one who called me a …"

I can't say it. Pete has no such problem.

"An Indian lover? If the shoe fits, wear it." I fall silent. Pete remarks, "I see you're not denying it."

PETE'S PA IS NOT pleased to see either one of us when at last Pete helps me to their cabin door. He's right about one thing—Mr. Harkness is all fired up about Pete taking the scow across the river in the dark. When Pete explains that he was worried something had happened to me, I get the feeling that in Dave Harkness's view, neither my life nor my limb qualifies as an emergency worth risking his ferry over.

Mrs. Bell calms Mr. Harkness down. She tells Jimmy to fetch some butter for the burn on my right hand, which has begun to throb something fierce, and she tells Pete to dish the two of us up some stew from the pot on the stove. She helps me off with my jacket and shirt so she can take a look at my injured left arm. She feels along my forearm, causing me to twinge.

"That's a break, right enough," she says in her Aussie twang. "You'll have to get Doc Thompson to set it in plaster."

"It can wait until the morning," declares Mr. Harkness.

She doesn't disagree with him, but fetches some rags she ties together to make a sling for my arm. Telling me to sit at the table, she takes the butter that Jimmy has brought and lathers it on my right hand. Pete puts a bowl of stew down before me. I'm famished, but with one arm in the sling and the other hand greased up, I have no way to pick up the spoon. Mrs. Bell sees my predicament, and smiles.

"Let me help you, luv," she says. She picks up the spoon and proceeds to feed me the stew. "Is that good?" she says, teasing me now. "Does Baby like his dinner?"

I am suddenly heated. I'm afraid I may be blushing. She smiles at the effect she's having on me.

"I think Baby likes it!" she declares in a sing-song voice.

She feeds me another spoonful, this time wiping gravy from my chin and licking it from her fingers. Now I feel stirrings in places one ought not to, especially not when those stirrings are caused by the more-or-less stepmother of your friend. I try to drive out the shameful thoughts she's started in me, to concentrate on the pain in my arm instead. I bow my head, praying that no one present will guess what's in my mind.

Pete gets up from the table, scraping his chair hard against the floor, breaking the spell she's cast over me.

"He can sleep upstairs in my bed," says Pete. "I'll sleep down here."

Mrs. Bell looks Pete in the eye, like she's amused by something.

"Don't worry, Pete," she says. "I won't bite him."

"He left the stew to burn!" Jimmy's suddenly shouting, his voice high and excited.

All eyes are on the stove now, where the big cast iron stew pot is sending up smoke. Mrs. Bell is across the room in half a second. She may be small, but she's strong—she grabs the handle with a cloth and swings the heavy pot onto the floor, all the while cursing Pete.

"Did you not think to add some water to it, you dimwit?!"

"He can't help it, Ma," says Jimmy. "He's just slow."

Pete looks like he'd like to drive his fist into Jimmy's plump, satisfied face. He answers back to Mrs. Bell, "Don't blame me! It was already burnt. Better to hide the taste!"

Mr. Harkness is across the room in a flash—cuffing Pete so hard against the side of his head that he sends him sprawling.

"Apologize to your mother!" he thunders.

Everybody's silent for a few seconds. It seems like

nobody's even breathing. Pete's still on the floor from the blow he just took from his pa. Slowly he gets up. I've never seen him like this—his face is red with fury, tears streaming down it.

"Goddamn you!" he says. He turns a look of pure hate on Mrs. Bell. "And goddamn her!"

Pete grabs his jacket from the hook and heads out into the night, slamming the door behind him. I'm sitting there wondering if I should follow him when Mrs. Bell turns to me and smiles.

"I reckon that settles it. You'll sleep in Pete's bed."

"Wipe that smirk off your face, boy." Mr. Harkness is speaking to Jimmy. "And don't you be calling Pete stupid."

Jimmy cowers a little and sidles closer to his mam. Mrs. Bell lifts her chin and gives Mr. Harkness a look that tells him to watch his step. He'll have to come through *her* if he wants to get his hands on Jimmy. I've never seen Dave Harkness back down before, but he does now.

I'm wondering where Pete has gone, and whether he's coming back. I'm wishing I was with him—anywhere but here, there's such a bad feeling in the room.

"If it's all right, I think I'll get to bed," I say. "Thank you for the stew, and for the sling."

Mrs. Bell lets out a hard laugh.

"You're a bit of a stuffed shirt, Georgie, but you're all right."

CHAPTER NINETEEN

AFTER BEING SO SLEEPY out on the trail, I think I
will never be able to fall asleep due to the throbbing
from my arm and my hand. But I must sleep, because
I wake up in darkness. At first I think I'm in my
own bed at home, but then the ache from my arm
makes me remember what happened. There's a curtain
covering a window beside my head, under which I
can see moonlight. I manage to shift enough to open
the curtain a little and let in more light. Now I can
see Jimmy sleeping in the other bed. I wonder if this
is the room that Joe Hampton and his brother slept
in when he lived here, before his father drowned. His
father must have built this house. It's a nice room,
with a window and all. The whole house is nice, nicer
than ours. If Mr. Hampton built it and it belonged
to him, I wonder why Agnes and her boys don't live
here still.

I hear voices from downstairs—Mrs. Bell and Mr.
Harkness, but I think I recognize Mr. Moultray's
voice, too. I wonder if Mr. Moultray knows where Pete

is. I ease myself out of bed and widen the crack in the open door just enough so I can slip through without waking Jimmy. The floorboards are cold against my stocking feet as I step to the top of the stairs. From here I can tell I was right—Mr. Moultray is in the parlor. He seems to be reading from a newspaper:

According to Indian agent Patrick McTiernan, who attended the gathering, the Indian chiefs hold William Osterman, a Nooksack man, responsible for the murder for which Louie Sam was lynched on the night of February 28.

The chiefs believe that Mr. Osterman, the local telegraph operator, lured Louie Sam to Nooksack on the pretext of employing him to repair the telegraph line. He asked the young Indian to walk with him toward the cabin of James Bell, the murdered man, only to then change his mind and tell him to 'go away.'

According to the chiefs, once Mr. Osterman was alone, he proceeded to the victim's cabin, committed the crime and made his getaway, correctly assuming that people would see Louie Sam near the cabin and blame him for the murder.

My heart is pounding by the time Mr. Moultray

stops reading. Are the chiefs right? Is it possible that Mr. Osterman is the murderer? But why? What did he have against Mr. Bell? I'm wondering why nobody is saying anything. Then Mr. Moultray speaks.

"You know how this looks, don't you? People are saying Jim Bell was planning on suing you."

Mrs. Bell speaks up. "Jim Bell was deranged. He told folks a lot of things that weren't true—most of them about me."

But it seems that Mr. Moultray meant the question for Mr. Harkness, not her.

"Dave," he says, "everybody knows that Bill Osterman's your brother-in-law, and your friend. Do you know something you're not telling me? Bill didn't have anything to do with this, did he?"

"Listen to Annette," says Mr. Harkness. "It's all lies. Those redskins are just looking for a reason to massacre us in our sleep."

"Goddamn it, answer my question! The governor's put out an order to find us. Just today there was a carrot top by the name of Clark snooping around the store." He must be talking about the red-headed man I saw at the hotel. "He was asking all sorts of questions about who led the posse, what I thought about the lynching …"

"What did you tell him?"

"As little as possible, which in and of itself was enough to tell him I was there." Mr. Moultray pauses before he asks, "Did Louie Sam kill Jim Bell, or not?"

"Why are you asking us?" says Mrs. Bell.

"Because I'm beginning to think you know more than you're saying. If we hung the wrong man, this could turn into a full-out Indian War."

"We did the right thing," says Mr. Harkness. "And don't you worry about no Indian War. If those thieving redskins make trouble, folks will come from as far away as Seattle to kill every one of them they can get their hands on. They're itching for the chance."

Says Mr. Moultray, "I'm the one who tightened the rope, goddammit!"

In my mind I'm back in that night, in that clearing. I see Mr. Moultray's startled look when Louie Sam recognizes him and speaks his name—I hear the slap he delivers to the pony's flank, sending it running. I see Louie Sam up in the air, legs kicking, fighting for his life to the very end.

Mrs. Bell speaks.

"That's right, Bill, you were the one—and don't you forget it. You've got a reputation to protect in this town. You've got ambitions. What's going to happen to your political career if you get arrested?"

"My question was for Dave, I'll thank you, Annette," says Mr. Moultray, "and he still hasn't answered it. Did you or Bill Osterman have anything to do with the death of Jim Bell?"

But Mrs. Bell answers him, her voice like a coiled

snake—hissing and ready to strike. "All you need to worry about," she says, "is keeping your gob shut."

"I'll take that as a yes," replies Mr. Moultray. He adds, his voice thick with emotion, "We killed an innocent boy."

Mrs. Bell hisses, "For God's sake, man. He was just an Indian."

I don't go back to sleep. How can I when my head's swimming from the things I've heard, from the memory of that clearing in the woods, of that night?

AT FIRST LIGHT I get up from Pete's bed and find my boots. Jimmy's snoring softly, his mouth hanging open. Between my broken arm and the burn on my right hand, it's a trick carrying my boots, but I manage to get down the stairs without waking any of the sleeping bodies in the house. I find my jacket on the hook by the door. The best I can manage is to drape it over my shoulders, like a shawl. Outside, I stick my feet into my boots. I'll have to wear them loose, without tying the laces. It's cold, but even if I had a way to pull on my mittens, my right hand is blistering and oozing from the burn, greasy from the butter Mrs. Bell slathered on it. I tuck it inside my jacket and start down the path to the river.

I am so relieved to be gone from that house that I feel light and happy, despite the ache from my arm—and despite the secrets I've heard. Why do the

Sumas chiefs think Mr. Osterman killed Mr. Bell? Is that what Louie Sam told them? I think back to the morning we found Mr. Bell dead in his cabin. Annie and I stayed behind while John and Will went to fetch the sheriff. Then Mr. Osterman showed up, saying he happened to be out checking the telegraph line. Is it possible he was lying? Was he in the neighborhood because *he* killed Mr. Bell and set the fire? Is Father right about his character? Is he a liar and a murderer, pretending to be a decent man? It seems Mr. Moultray has his doubts about him, too.

I shudder at the thought of looking Bill Osterman in the eye to ask for my wages, but I'll have to do it. I promised Mrs. Thompson I'd pay for Teddy's medicine today. And then I'll have to pay Dr. Thompson to set my arm in plaster. My happy feeling is gone. I feel sick inside.

I reach Mr. Moultray's livery stable, down the track from the ferry dock. It's so early, not even Jack Simpson is up and about. I have an inkling that I might find Pete inside. If it was me, that's where I would go to find shelter for the night. The horses stir in their stalls when I go inside, thinking I have their breakfast with me.

"Pete?" I whisper. I don't know why I'm whispering. I suppose all the secret talk has got me on edge. "Pete?"

"Here." I follow the sound of his voice to an empty stall, where he's made himself a bed out of straw and a horse blanket. I woke him up. He's grumpy. "What are you doing out so early?" he asks.

"I'm going into town."

"To see Doc Thompson?"

"To see your uncle, for my money."

Pete grunts a reply.

"Mr. Moultray paid a visit last night," I tell him.

"What did he want?"

"He wanted to know if it's true what the Sumas are saying, that your uncle's the one who murdered Mr. Bell."

If yesterday I had accused his kin of murder, Pete would have hauled off and hit me. But this morning, a look of confusion comes over his face.

"Why would anybody pay any mind to what the Sumas have got to say?" he grumbles.

"Mr. Moultray is paying mind to it. He asked your pa straight out if he knows anything about Bill Osterman murdering Mr. Bell."

Pete has no answer to that.

"Your pa didn't deny it."

For a moment, he locks eyes with me. I see how afraid he is.

"Pete, what do you know?"

The moment is over. I've pushed him too far. He rolls over away from me and pulls the horse blanket up over his shoulder.

"It's too early for so much talking."

That's it—that's all I'm going to get out of him. But I tell him, thinking it might make him feel better, "After you left, your pa told Jimmy to shut his trap about you."

He's silent for a moment or two. His back is to me, so I don't know whether he's sleeping, or thinking. Then he says, "I won't be able to go get that saw for you. I can't get across the river. I'm not going near him today."

"That's okay. Thanks, anyway," I tell him.

"I'll see you, George."

"I'll see you, Pete."

At that I head out of the stable. Once again I'm happy to be out in the fresh air, away from the trapped feeling I get around the Harknesses, father and son.

Chapter Twenty

It's still early when I get to town, and all
the businesses are closed up tight, including Dr.
Thompson's drug store. I go into the Nooksack Hotel
even though I know the telegraph office is likely
to be closed, too, and I'm right. Two days ago I felt
shy about asking Mr. Hopkins if I could wait in the
lobby for Mr. Osterman, but today the ache in my
arm makes me not care. There's a plain wood bench
near the door. I sit down on it, thinking that Mr.
Hopkins can't complain about my dirty clothes the
way he would if I sat myself on the fancy upholstered
furniture. He's eyeing me from behind his desk.

"The telegraph office doesn't open until nine,"
he says.

"I'll wait, thank you," I reply.

I'm not sitting there for five minutes when who
should come down the spiral staircase from his room
but the red-headed man, the one Mr. Moultray called
by the name of Clark. I guess I'm staring at him,
because suddenly Carrot Top is looking at me. I turn

my head away, but not fast enough. He ambles over and sits down at the other end of my bench, although he has his pick of places to sit in the empty lobby.

"I saw you in here the other day, didn't I?" he says. His accent sounds Irish. "You said you were working for Mr. Osterman."

"Yes, sir."

There's something about him that's making me uneasy. I keep looking straight ahead, making it clear that I don't want to talk. But that doesn't stop him.

"You seem kind of young for a telegraph man."

To which I say nothing. He nods at my arm in the sling.

"Dangerous work, from the look of it. What did he hire you to do?"

"To check the line."

"That's a big job."

"Yes, sir."

"Is that how you got hurt?"

"Yes, sir."

Mr. Moultray was right about one thing: this fella Clark asks a lot of questions. From the corner of my eye I can see Mr. Hopkins glancing over at us. He seems nervous.

"How long have you worked for Mr. Osterman?" says Carrot Top. "I ask because I heard he was going to hire another boy a couple of weeks ago."

I answer, "I don't know anything about that."

I'm lying. Of course I know that Louie Sam expected Mr. Osterman to hire him, but Mr. Moultray told us never to speak about Louie Sam and there's something about the way Mr. Hopkins is staring at us now from the hotel desk that is warning me to be careful.

This Mr. Clark won't give up.

"You don't know how long you've worked for him," he says, "or you don't know about the other boy?"

"About the other boy," I reply.

He takes out a tobacco pouch and tucks a chew into his mouth. The tobacco makes a bulge inside his cheek. I can see he plans to sit here for a while yet.

"That boy met an unfortunate end, of course. I'm sure you heard about it." I say nothing. "I hear tell that there were a couple of white boys about his age who rode up to Canada with the lynch mob. Might you know who those boys were? I ask because there are only so many boys around Nooksack, and I presume that you all go to school together. I can imagine that a couple of kids going on an adventure like that might want to boast about it the next day. Did you hear any ballyhoo like that around the schoolyard?"

"No," I say.

I get to my feet. I have to get away from this man.

"You're George Gillies, aren't you?" he says. That stops me. "I talked to your father yesterday. He said you were off helping Mr. Osterman." He smiles kindly, like I'm supposed to take him for a friend. "There's no cause to be frightened, George. I'm just trying to find out what exactly happened that night."

"Why do you want to know?" I ask. "Who are you?"

"My name is Arthur Clark. I've been sent here by the Dominion Government to investigate the lynching."

"I don't know anything about it."

I'm a liar and a coward, but I don't want to go to jail. He seems to read my mind.

"Understand that the only people who are in trouble with the law are the ones who led the mob. A boy who just happened to tag along, he could go a long way toward easing his conscience if he helped bring justice for the native boy who was killed."

Should I trust him? I stand there like a dumb fool trying to decide. Pete Harkness and I might be all right, but what about Father? Would they consider him a leader? He could be arrested. Mr. Clark sees me weakening.

"I talked to a friend of yours yesterday, George. Young Pete Harkness."

This is news to me. Why didn't Pete say anything to me about being questioned by Mr. Clark?

"He told me about running into Louie Sam on the road from Lynden. Got a colorful way of describing the Indian boy. Makes him sound most fearsome. It's quite a story."

I've got a bad feeling about where this is going, like

this Clark fella has read my mind again.

"Did Pete ever talk to you privately about that, George?" says the Canadian Government man. "Did he ever let it slip that maybe somebody *suggested* to him that he saw Louie Sam? That somebody told Pete how to describe him to make him sound like he could have just come from murdering Mr. Bell? Like, for instance, his uncle, Mr. Osterman?"

That settles it—this man *is* a mind reader!

"I got to be going," I say.

"I'll tell you what, George," says Mr. Clark. "I'll be staying here for a few more days. You know where to find me if you think of anything that might help. Fair enough?"

Speak of the devil, who should walk into the hotel at that very moment but Mr. Osterman? He looks from me to Mr. Clark. He is not pleased to see that we've been conversing. I want to tell him that it was Mr. Clark doing all the talking, not me. I'm afraid of him as I have never been before.

"What happened to your arm, George?"

"I fell," I say. "The wire at pole number fifty-one was hanging loose. I tried to put it back up."

"Seems you sent a boy to do a man's job, Mr. Osterman."

"I believe I told you yesterday, Mr. Clark, that I have nothing more to say to you."

Mr. Clark smiles pleasantly.

"There's no law against me talking to George here, is there?"

There is no humor in Mr. Osterman when he replies. "I'd be careful about talking so much. You wouldn't want to catch a throat disease."

Mr. Clark isn't smiling now, either.

"Are you threatening me?"

"Think of it more as good advice."

Mr. Clark takes a couple of chews of his tobacco, then gets up slowly, like he's got all the time in the world. He sends a stream of brown juice into the brass spittoon in the corner. He turns back to Mr. Osterman, like at last he's thought of a reply.

"Then I suppose I should thank you for it."

"Mind your business, Mr. Clark."

"An unlawful act took place in Canadian territory, Mr. Osterman. The Dominion Government has the cooperation of your government to discover the true circumstances of that act. That makes it my business."

With that, Mr. Clark heads outdoors. Mr. Osterman sizes me up.

"What did you tell him?"

"Nothing!"

"Make sure you keep it that way."

He unlocks the door to the telegraph office and goes inside. I follow him.

"Mr. Osterman?"

"What?" he snaps.

"I need my wages, for yesterday."

"You were supposed to put in a full day. You only got to pole fifty-one."

Does he not see that my arm is in a sling, and that I'm in pain?

"I got hurt," I say.

"Through your own stupidity. Nobody told you to go climbing the poles."

"You told me to fix them. That's what I was trying to do."

He sees the burn on my right hand.

"What happened there?"

"I was trying to put the line back on the insulator."

"Don't you know enough to know the wire is electrified? You're lucky you didn't bring the whole line down."

He's trying to make me feel ignorant and small, but instead I feel angry.

"How was I supposed to know?" I ask. "You didn't tell me."

"Don't talk back to me, boy," he says.

He reaches into his pocket for a handful of coins and picks out three bits. He throws them at me. There's no way I can catch them with my injuries.

"There. Now get out of my sight."

The coins bounce off the floor, scattering. I'm burning up with anger and shame as I kneel down to pick them up.

"This is only half of what I'm owed," I tell him.

"You did half a day's work. You get paid for half a day."

"But—"

"Get!" he says, raising his voice. "And don't let me see you around here again."

Mr. Osterman is a villain through and through, I have no doubt of that now. My first thought is to find Mr. Clark and tell him everything I know. I head outside and scan the street for him. But instead of Mr. Clark, my eyes fix on the one man I have more to fear from at this moment than Mr. Osterman. I see Father across the street, coming out of the drug store with Dr. Thompson.

CHAPTER TWENTY-ONE

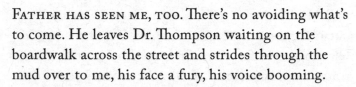

FATHER HAS SEEN ME, TOO. There's no avoiding what's
to come. He leaves Dr. Thompson waiting on the
boardwalk across the street and strides through the
mud over to me, his face a fury, his voice booming.

"George, where the hell have you been? Your mam's
worried sick."

"I spent the night at the Harknesses'," I say.

"What happened to your arm?"

"It's broken. I had a fall." The tears I've been holding back burst forth. I'm crying like a little kid, snot
running from my nose. "I lost your saw. I'm sorry!"

"My saw?" Father's staring at me, puzzled, trying
to make sense of what I'm saying. He looks tired and
worn, like this is the last straw. He opens my right
hand in his and examines the burn on my palm. "How
did this happen?"

"It got burned by the electricity in the wire."

"What were you doing touching the wire? Did
Mam not tell ye to be careful?"

"I didn't know!" I say. Suddenly, I'm in a confessing

mood. "I only got seventy-five cents," I say, wiping the snot on my sleeve. "Half of what I'm owed. Mr. Osterman says not to come back."

Father's jaw sets. "Does he now?" He looks up toward the telegraph office. "Wait here," he tells me, and heads into the hotel.

But I follow him inside. I get to the telegraph office door in time to see Father pulling Mr. Osterman up out of his swivel chair by his jacket.

"Give the boy what he's owed, you no-account bastard!" he thunders.

Mr. Osterman is younger and stronger than Father, but Father is fierce. I'd be lying if I said I'm not pleased to see Mr. Osterman cowering, but I'm surprised that Father is so worked up about my wages.

"Easy," says Mr. Osterman.

"You sent a young boy out to tend the line without so much as a speck of training! Were you hoping he'd get killed? Is that it? Another boy dead?"

Mr. Hopkins pushes past me into the office.

"Break it up! You want that detective to hear?"

Mr. Hopkins is a shrimp. Father could take him easily, but he doesn't put up a fight. The rage has gone out of him. He gives Mr. Osterman a hateful look.

"Somebody ought to stand up to you," he says.

"Don't try putting yourself above the rest of us, Gillies," says Osterman. "We were all there. We were all agreed."

Mr. Hopkins speaks up. "We did what was necessary."

I want to shout out that he's wrong, that Louie Sam didn't murder Mr. Bell—that the real murderer is standing right here before us. But my courage fails me.

"The choice is simple," says Bill Osterman. "Stand together or fall separately."

Father seems to shrink a little at that. He turns and sees me in the doorway. There's that same look in his eyes I saw that night, when he told me to be quiet about the suspenders. I couldn't put a name to it then, but now I can. It's shame. My father is ashamed. As much as I sometimes fear his temper, to see him belittled so is more frightening. I need him to be strong. I need him to be right—the way he was right about us having a better life in America than the one we left behind in Great Britain. The way he was right that he'd be free to be his own man, and we boys after him.

Osterman digs in his pants for more coins, the rest of my pay. He opens my jacket pocket and drops them inside.

"Take it," he says, "and get out. The pair of you."

Mr. Hopkins goes back to his desk without another word to us. Father and I leave the telegraph office like kicked dogs. When we're outside of the hotel, I tell him, "Not everyone is with Mr. Osterman. Abigail Stevens says her pa thinks you were right."

"Right about what?"

"About letting the Canadian law deal with Louie Sam."

"You're not to talk about that."

"How can we not talk about it?"

"Quiet, George."

It's only when we start across the street that I see Mae hitched to our wagon. The fact that it's just Mae and not Ulysses, too, can mean only one thing: Father was in a hurry to get to town. Dr. Thompson is seated on the wagon bench, holding his medical bag on his lap. He's cross at being kept waiting.

"I thought you said this was an emergency," he says.

"My apologies, Doctor," replies Father.

"Is it Teddy?" I ask him.

"Aye."

He offers nothing more, but I know that it's serious if he's come to fetch Dr. Thompson. Father climbs up beside the doctor and takes Mae's reins, while I prop myself up in the flatbed at the back.

"It appears you have another patient," Father remarks.

Dr. Thompson half turns his bulk around to get a look at me, the largeness of his belly making it awkward for him to do so.

"I'm all right," I say. Then, "I have your money."

"What money might that be?"

"What we owe you for the medicine."

I feel for the coins in my jacket pocket. The burn on my hand means I'm only able to grasp them with my fingertips. They keep slipping away. Father snaps the reins across Mae's hindquarters and she starts off, making the wagon lurch and jarring my sore arm. Without meaning to, I let out a cry.

"Broken, I warrant," pronounces Dr. Thompson. "Stop the wagon. I'll need plaster of Paris from the store."

"The bairn needs you more," says Father. "He's burning up."

So Teddy's fever has returned. Mam must be mad with worry. Father whips the reins, working Mae up to a fast trot, making the wagon pitch and jiggle—sending pain shooting through my arm with every hoofbeat. But I tell myself it's penance for my cowardly ways, for the shame that Father and I have brought upon ourselves. I send a silent prayer to God promising that if only he'll spare Teddy, I'll go talk to Carrot Top Clark, and I'll tell him what evil Bill Osterman has brought upon us all.

MAE HAS WORKED UP a lather by the time we head up the track to our cabin. Gyp comes barking to meet us, but otherwise the house is silent as Father pulls Mae to a halt in the yard. There's no crying of a sick baby to be heard. None of us says anything about it, but I'll wager we're all in fear that Teddy has stopped taking breaths with which to cry. Will comes outside at the sound of the wagon.

"John ran off!" he says, eager to deliver his news. "He's gone to fetch Agnes, though Mam told him not to, because the doctor is coming."

Father is not pleased, but I'm thinking that there can't be any harm in fetching Agnes. She's the one who brought Teddy into the world, after all. With some effort, Dr. Thompson shifts his weight around in the wagon seat to get two feet on the ground.

"Where's the patient?" he asks.

Inside the cabin, Mam has got Teddy in a tub of water on the table, trying to bring his fever down. When she sees me walk in behind Dr. Thompson and Father, her eyes light up and for a brief second the furrows of worry leave her face. Then she's angry.

"I'll deal with you later," she says.

She lifts the baby out of the water and wraps him in a blanket. Anybody can see how skinny and still he is, how uninterested in being alive.

"Good God, woman," says Dr. Thompson. "Have you been starving this child?"

"When I try to nurse him, he falls asleep after a thimble full," Mam tells him. "I've tried cow's milk. He doesn't want that, either. But I give him his medicine, three times a day just like you said to do."

"Let me have a look, then."

Mam lays the baby gently on the table and steps

aside so that Dr. Thompson can get a look at him. The doctor sets his bag on a chair and takes from it his wooden listening tube. He tells Mam, "Unswaddle the infant, please."

Mam lifts the blanket away and Dr. Thompson puts the tip of the tube to Teddy's tiny chest and the earpiece to his own ear. He listens for what seems a long, long time, with all of us —Father and Mam, Will, Annie, Isabel, and me—watching him frown and purse his lips. Teddy fusses a little, not liking the listening tube. At last Dr. Thompson pulls back from the baby. For a second, he won't look at Mam. When he does, we can all see in his face that there's no hope. Mam buckles a little. She grabs hold of a chair back to steady herself. Father steps over to her, and takes her elbow in his hand.

"His lungs are very weak," says Dr. Thompson. "For whatever reason, this baby has failed to thrive. I'm sorry. There is nothing to be done for him."

CHAPTER TWENTY-TWO

MAM DOESN'T CRY, BUT I know inside she wants to.
She bundles little Teddy up in the blanket and holds
him tight against her, able to speak but half a thought.

"But the medicine …"

"I'm sorry," says Dr. Thompson. "You've left it too
late. Perhaps if you had brought him to me sooner."

I hate the way he's making Mam feel that what's
wrong with Teddy is all her fault. I can't help myself. I
have to speak up.

"We brought him but two weeks ago," I say. "Don't
you remember? You said the medicine would make
him better, but he just kept getting sicker."

"Silence," says Father, but not in an angry way. I'm
thinking he may agree with me.

"Medicine is not a precise science," huffs the
doctor. "Naturally, I hoped the baby would improve,
but I don't claim to work miracles. Now," he says,
turning to Father, "if you will be so kind as to
transport me back into town, I have other patients
to see."

"What about George's arm?" says Father.

Dr. Thompson looks over at me like I'm fly speck for questioning him.

"Save your money and put a splint on it yourself. That will do as well as a plaster cast," he says.

He's talking like we Gillies are paupers. That makes me even madder.

"Will," I say. "Reach into my pocket. You'll find six bits in there." Will fishes into my pocket and brings out the six coins. "Those are for you," I say to the doctor.

Will hands Dr. Thompson the money. He jingles the coins in his palm, like he's trying to see if they're real. He gives me a false smile and says, "Thank you, son." Then, to Father, "I'll be sure to tell Mrs. Thompson that your account is settled." He nods his head at Mam. "Good day, Mrs. Gillies. I wish I had been able to give you better news."

Mam sits in the rocking chair once Father and Dr. Thompson are gone, cuddling Teddy and singing to him softly.

Across the room, Annie asks me, "Is Teddy going to die, George?"

"That's up to God's will," I say, loud enough so Mam can hear. "The best thing we can do is look after ourselves so Mam can look after him."

"Does your arm hurt much?"

"Yes. Is there any breakfast left?"

I feel guilty for thinking of my stomach at a time like this, but I haven't eaten since last night and I am ravenous. Mam calls from the rocker,

"Fix George some bread and jam, Annie."

"Yes, Mam."

"We'll see to your arm once you've eaten, George."

Little Isabel has had enough of being good. She holds out her skirt and begins twirling around the room.

"Annie, let's dance," she says.

"Not now!"

Annie is busy slicing bread for me, using her bossy tone to warn Isabel that she has more important duties to perform than playing with her. Isabel keeps dancing, twirling faster and making herself dizzy. She knocks a chair, but keeps on going. "Isabel, stop!" says Annie.

"But I want to dance!"

You can see it's only a matter of time before she bumps her head and starts crying. Ordinarily Mam would be telling Isabel to mind Annie, but Mam is only gazing at her from the rocker, shiny-eyed.

"Isabel!"

Annie is cross at not being obeyed. She grabs hold of Isabel by the arm to stop her. I can see that Isabel is winding up to a howl of protest. I'm not usually one to get mixed up with child-minding—that's women's work—but I find myself saying, "I'll dance with her."

Isabel lights up. Annie retreats to the cutting board,

where she spreads jam on bread for me. I hold out the uninjured fingers of my right hand. Isabel reaches up with her tiny hand and grasps them. Together we begin swaying in a waltz around the room. I'm careful to keep the sling holding my broken arm close to my side.

"You're a good dancer, George," says Isabel.

Looking down at her plump face framed by curls, I dip my head to her in a little bow.

"Thank you kindly, Miss. So are you."

Mam's watching us from the rocker, smiling. I hold up Isabel's hand with mine to allow her to pirouette. That's what Mam calls it when she spins. Will brings an armful of wood in from outside and carries it to the stove, looking at me like I've lost my mind, but I don't care. It's at that moment that John comes in, followed by Agnes. Agnes laughs at the sight of Isabel and me.

"*To'ke–tie!*" she says.

Then her glance falls on Teddy, and her smile disappears.

AGNES TAKES OVER, and we let her. First she makes Will understand between Chinook and her little bit of English to fill a pot of water at the creek and to start it boiling on the stove. From her beaded bag she takes a bundle of dried herbs and hands them to Annie, who looks confused.

"*Ee'-na stick.* Tea," Agnes says. "For *waum sick.*"

I know that "*stick*" serves general purpose for "wood" in Chinook jargon, and as I look closer at the dried bundle I see that it's leaves from a willow tree. I can guess what "*waum sick*" means.

"She wants you to make willow tea to bring down Teddy's fever," I tell Annie.

Agnes goes to Mam and reaches for the baby. You can see that Mam doesn't want to give him up, but she knows Agnes is his only hope. Agnes gently takes him into her arms. Smiling and cooing at Teddy in her own Sumas tongue, she unfolds the blanket and takes a good look at him. We're all watching her close, just as we did with Dr. Thompson not half an hour ago. It's hard to read what she's thinking. At last she asks, "*Ik-tah muck'-a-muck? To-toosh?*" I'm shocked by her immodesty as she puts her hand over one of her bosoms, in case we don't understand. "Milk?" she says in English.

"He never seems hungry," replies Mam. "More often than not, he refuses. When he does nurse, he throws the milk back up."

Agnes looks puzzled. She puts her fingers to her mouth, like she's putting food there.

"*Weght?*" she says. Then, in English, "More food?"

John pipes up, "She wants to know if he's been eating anything else besides milk."

Mam starts to shake her head. Then she remembers, "The medicine."

John fetches the bottle of Dr. Thompson's medicine from the shelf beside the stove. Agnes passes the baby back to Mam and pulls out the cork stopper to take a whiff of what's inside. Her nose wrinkles. Then her look is pure disgust.

"Baby *páht-lum!*" she says.

None of us knows what she means.

"What's *páht-lum?*" I ask.

Agnes does a crazy dance, making her eyes roll. I can't believe it. Mam is aghast.

"Are you saying my baby is *drunk?*"

Agnes nods. She speaks the next word slowly and carefully, like she's trying to teach it to us. "Laud-um." She repeats, "Laud-um."

I'm at a loss. It's no Chinook word I've ever heard of. But Mam understands.

"Laudanum," she says. "You mean there's laudanum in the medicine."

Agnes nods her head, expecting Mam to get her drift, but she doesn't.

"Of course there's laudanum in it," says Mam. "It's medicine."

Agnes seems upset by our confusion. She prattles off something in Sumas lingo. We stare at her, then we look to each other. It's one thing for Dr. Thompson's medicine not to be doing Teddy any good, but is she saying it's making him drunk?

"What's wrong with laudanum?" I ask.

Agnes tilts her head and rests it on her hands, held together. She closes her eyes.

"Baby *moo'-sum*. Make sleep."

I can see the truth dawning on Mam's face.

"The medicine's been making him too sleepy! That's why he isn't interested in feeding. That's why he won't gain weight."

Agnes gives three nods of her head, relieved that at last we slow-pokes have caught on. Holding it like poison, Mam takes the bottle from Agnes and thrusts it at John.

"Pour it down the privy!" she declares.

She holds Teddy to her like he'll be safe as long as he's in her arms.

CHAPTER TWENTY-THREE

WHEN FATHER GETS BACK and hears what's happened, he sends Agnes home with a twenty-pound sack of our best flour, which he has John carry for her. Before she leaves, she makes Mam understand that she's to let the baby suck on cloth that's been soaked in willow tea as much as he's willing. All of us know that little Teddy is not out of the woods, but now at least we have hope for him.

Father has bought plaster of Paris from Dr. Thompson. He gets Annie to cut up some old gunnysacks into strips, and he tells Will to bring him an old sock from Mam's sewing basket—one that already has holes in the toe. He cuts the toe open and slips the tube that results over my broken forearm. While he mixes the plaster with water, he tells me to sit at the table and has me hold my arm bent halfway at the elbow, with my palm upward. He dips the strips of burlap into the plaster mixture and begins winding them around the sock.

"How do you know this is right?" I ask him.

"I've not been a farmer all my life without learning how to set a broken bone," he replies, pretending to be offended. He's almost jovial, so lightened is his mood by our hope for the baby.

He takes another strip and dips it, squeezing it between his thumb and fingers until there's just the right amount of plaster on it. He winds it around my arm from where the last piece left off. Just when I'm thinking that I can't remember the last time I sat in such companionable silence with my Father, he says, "About that saw."

I bow my head.

"Why did you not ask me if you could borrow it?"

There's nothing for it but to speak the truth.

"I was afraid."

"Afraid I'd say no?"

"Afraid … because I thought you didn't want me to go work for Mr. Osterman."

He nods, and applies another strip of plastered burlap.

"I'll buy you a new one," I say.

"You spent everything you had on the doctor's bill."

"I'll earn more."

"Not from Mr. Osterman."

I want to tell him what I've learned about the telegraph man and the part it seems he played in Mr. Bell's murder, but the children and Mam are about.

"No, sir. Not from him."

After a long moment, he says, "Let's call it even, shall we? The doctor's bill for the saw."

I catch his gaze. He's looking at me man to man. That makes me feel good, better than I have felt in all these last two weeks. I keep my voice low.

"Father, do you know what the Sumas are saying about Mr. Osterman?"

"Aye."

"Do you believe it?"

He takes his time answering.

"Nobody has proof," he says. "At least, no white man. Without proof, he'll go on as he is."

I think about this as Father continues to apply plaster to my arm. What proof *is* there? I try to remember every detail of the morning we found the body. I recall that Mr. Osterman looked shocked enough by the sight of the bloody hole in the back of Mr. Bell's head, but that could have been play-acting. I remember he tried to talk me into taking Annie home, telling me that he would wait for the sheriff to arrive. When I refused, he told me to go wait with Annie by the track. How long did Annie and I wait? A quarter of an hour? A half? Time enough for Mr. Osterman to arrange things around the cabin for his own purposes. And he was the one who suggested we follow that trail into the swamp, where we found the broken branches and the tinned food and the suspenders. Did he plant them there, and lead us to them?

When I went to Mr. Osterman asking to do the job he was thinking about hiring Louie Sam to do, it was like he'd forgotten that job ever existed. Not only that, but he sent me to repair the other end of the line—the opposite end from the one that supposedly needed fixing. So ... did the poles near Mr. Bell's cabin never really need fixing? Did he draw Louie Sam to Nooksack with the promise of work, when his real purpose was to make it look like *he* was the one who killed the old man? Did Mr. Osterman let all of us believe that Louie Sam killed Mr. Bell—nay, *lead* us to believe it—to keep suspicion away from himself?

These are the thoughts that fill my head. By the time Father has finished with my arm, I am resolved that Bill Osterman must face justice.

MAM SENDS ME TO bed early, and I sleep like a log. I wake up before dawn to the sound of Teddy crying. It's a good sound. The cast on my arm is heavy and still a little damp, but the constant pain has simmered down to a dull ache. Pulling on my trousers with one hand, I go out from the bedroom to find Mam walking the floor with Teddy bundled in her arms. He's shrieking and frantic. Mam looks worn out. I wonder when she last had a full night's sleep.

"How is he?" I ask.

"His fever's gone down," she says.

Father comes out from the space he and Mam share behind the curtain, pulling up his suspenders.

"Is he hungry?"

"I fed him not a half hour ago!"

She puts the baby into Father's arms. Teddy wails all the louder, thrashing his little arms. Father tries to calm him, but he hasn't Mam's touch. Mam settles herself in the rocker and begins opening her blouse—all modesty gone! I turn my back away. But in another moment, the baby has stopped crying. I hear the snuffling sound of him sucking.

"You'd think he'd never been offered the breast before," says Father.

"Aye," says Mam. I can hear the smile in her voice. "He's making up for lost time."

CHAPTER TWENTY-FOUR

MAM REMINDS ME IT IS Tuesday morning, and there's
school. Despite my broken arm and despite the upset
in our house, she insists that John, Will, Annie, and
I will not miss another day of learning. She gets no
argument from me. I have my own reasons for making
the trek into Nooksack, but they have naught to do
with Miss Carmichael making me recite the sonnets
of Mr. Shakespeare for the umpteenth time. I have
not forgotten that at the moment I laid eyes on Father
outside the Nooksack Hotel yesterday morning, I was
on my way to see Mr. Clark, the detective sent by the
Dominion Government to investigate the hanging of
Louie Sam. I make a vow to myself that I will find
him this morning to tell him what I know.

But I'm afraid of how Mr. Osterman might
get back at Father and me if I tell Mr. Clark what
happened that night, knowing as I now do what
a villain Mr. Osterman is. He tricked the men of
Nooksack into executing an innocent boy. I wish
I'd listened to my niggling feeling the night Louie

Sam died. I wish I'd spoken up about the suspenders. Maybe some of those men would have listened. But all I can do for Louie Sam is speak up now.

AS WE WALK PAST Mr. Bell's burnt-out place on our way to the schoolhouse in town, Will says we should hurry up or Mr. Bell's ghost will grab hold of us by the ankles and pull us into the swamp to drown us.

"Stop talking nonsense," says John.

"It's true!" claims Will. "Arthur Breckenridge says Tom was walking Mary Hecht home past here after the dance at Moultray's on Friday night, when all of a sudden she starts getting pulled into the swamp and he has to save her."

"More likely Tom and Mary got caught smooching in the bushes and had to make up a story," replies John.

"You boys mind your tongues around Annie," says I, mindful of preserving my sister's innocence.

"I know what smooching is!" Annie declares, all miffed.

John gets a smirk.

"Then maybe you should tell George what smooching is, Annie. Abigail Stevens would thank you for it."

If I had a good arm and a hand that wasn't burnt, I'd wallop John so hard he wouldn't know what hit him. But I don't, so instead I hook his left leg with my right foot and send him sprawling into the muddy track. He springs to his feet again.

"Damn you, George," he cusses, causing Annie to cover up her ears. "If you weren't crippled, I'd settle this right here and now."

"Shut your gob, John," says I. "I have no time for such childishness."

John spews damnation at me for calling him a child. I quicken my pace and walk ahead on my own with John still yelling at me. I have no patience this morning. I'm thinking about exactly what I'm going to say to Mr. Clark when I find him. I know what he wants— the names of those who led the Nooksack Vigilance Committee up the Whatcom Trail to Canada. I have no hesitation naming Mr. Osterman, sure as I am now that he set this whole tragedy in motion. I have my suspicions about Dave Harkness being in on it, too. But what about Mr. Moultray and Mr. Breckenridge and Mr. Hopkins? Weren't they misled by Mr. Osterman, just as much as the rest of us were?

My head is so full up with thinking that I am not aware that Abigail is waiting for me at the gate to Stevens's sawmill up ahead until I am almost upon her.

"George, what happened to your arm?"

I think about telling her that I suffered an injury while doing important work on the telegraph line, but instead I find myself stating plain and simple, "I fell out of a tree."

"Well, that was a stupid thing to do," says she.

I am coming to admire Abigail's way with the unvarnished truth—despite the fact that her unvarnished truths usually have something to do with one failing of mine or another. We fall in walking together toward school, Abigail holding her school books up against her front like she might need them for protection.

"How was the dance?" I ask her.

"I wouldn't know."

"What do you mean?"

"When Mr. Pratt started up his fiddle, Mrs. Bell and Pete's pa were the first ones on the dance floor. My ma took one look at that floozy showing herself off like the belle of Whatcom County and made Pa take me and my little sisters directly home."

"From the way Mrs. Bell parades around town, seems like she and a few others think they run the place," I remark.

"You're talking about Mr. Osterman, aren't you?" she says.

That throws me a little. What does Abigail know about Mr. Osterman?

"What makes you say that?"

"Everybody knows what the Indians are saying about him killing Mr. Bell."

"Do people believe it?"

"'Course not. Who's going to believe a bunch of

Indians against the word of a white man?"

"Do you believe them?"

A rare occurrence happens. For several moments, Abigail says nothing at all. When she finally speaks, it's without her usual spit and fire.

"If I tell you something, you promise to keep it secret?" she says.

"I promise."

"The morning that Mr. Bell was murdered, Pa saw Mr. Osterman with the Indian boy. They were walking out of town, toward Mr. Bell's place."

I can't believe Mr. Stevens has kept this to himself all this time.

"What were they doing? Were they talking? Were they arguing?"

"They weren't fighting or talking. They were just walking. But here's the thing."

"What?"

"Louie Sam wasn't carrying a rifle, at least not that Pa could see. So how did he shoot Mr. Bell?"

I'm staggered by this news. It's exactly the way the Sumas say it happened—Mr. Osterman got Louie Sam to walk with him as far as Mr. Bell's place to make it look like Louie Sam was the murderer.

"Why didn't your pa tell anybody about it?" I ask.

"Same reason nobody says anything out loud. Because they're afraid of what might happen to them as a result."

"Somebody's got to stand up," I say.

"George Gillies, you just got finished promising me you wouldn't say a word!"

She's got me in a corner. It's one thing to work up my own courage to do the right thing and tell what I know, but a promise is a promise.

"I won't say anything," I tell her.

Abigail looks me in the eye. For once she isn't mocking me or teasing me. She's dead serious.

"The only reason I told you is because I know I can trust you, George."

I'm amazed by how a few nice words from Abigail can make me feel so warm all over. I say, "I gave you my word, and I mean it."

We've reached the point in town where the trail widens out to become Nooksack Avenue. Abigail starts down the path toward the schoolhouse. I have another destination in mind.

"I'll see you at school, Abigail."

"Where might you be going?" she asks, all sassy once more.

"Never you mind. Tell Miss Carmichael I'll be along directly."

"I'll be sure to give her the message," she says.

She's being sarcastic. I can see we're back to normal, she and I.

"Thank you kindly," I answer back without batting an eye, pleased with myself that I'm learning to hold

216

my own with her.

Abigail gives me a smile as we part ways. With that I set out down Nooksack Avenue, heading for the Nooksack Hotel—wondering how I'm going to tell Carrot Top about what Mr. Stevens saw, without breaking my promise to Abigail.

CHAPTER TWENTY-FIVE

"MR. CLARK IS GONE," says Mr. Hopkins, "and if
you're smart, you'll be gone out of here, too, before
anybody finds out you came in here looking for him."

I'm standing in the lobby of the Nooksack Hotel.
From the way Mr. Hopkins is nodding toward the
telegraph office, I know he's warning me about the
consequences of Mr. Osterman finding out I've come
looking for the detective. But having worked up my
courage this far, I'm not prepared to be put off now.

"Mr. Clark told me he'd be here for a few days," I say.

"He was persuaded to change his plans," replies Mr.
Hopkins.

The way he says it, I get the feeling that Mr. Clark
was not persuaded in the nicest way.

"Who persuaded him?" I ask.

"Look, George," says Mr. Hopkins, stabbing
his finger in my direction, "if you know what's
good for you and yours, you'll stop asking so many
damn questions. Or you'll find out for yourself who
persuaded him."

It doesn't matter. I already know the answer. I saw for myself Mr. Osterman making threats against Mr Clark right here in the lobby yesterday morning. At that point, Mr. Clark was sounding brave and resolute, but I'm guessing that Mr. Osterman found a way to bring him down a notch or two.

"Did Mr. Clark leave word where he can be reached?" I ask.

"Why don't you try sending him a telegram?" says Mr. Hopkins. "I'm sure Mr. Osterman would be much obliged to transmit it for you."

Seems there's a sarcasm epidemic going on in this town. Remembering my manners, I thank him anyway and head out into the street—glad at least for the good fortune that I have not had to face Mr. Osterman this morning.

THERE'S NOTHING FOR IT but to head over to the schoolhouse. Owing to my failure to find Mr. Clark, it turns out that I am there in good time before Miss Carmichael rings the bell to call us inside. Abigail glances over to me from where she's talking with some of the other girls, then looks away just as quickly. I understand that she's not mad or ignoring me. It's just that, here in the schoolyard, we're one way together. Outside … it seems that maybe we're starting to be another way.

I see Pete Harkness over in the corner of the yard

talking tough with some of the older fellas, including Tom Breckenridge. I head over to him. It's not until I get close that I see the shiner on his right eye. I remember him telling me early yesterday morning he was planning on staying out of his pa's way for fear of his temper. My first thought is that he did not succeed. But he's telling the boys around him a different story altogether.

"… when this drunken Paddy come off the ferry complaining the ride was too rough, I tell him he can go eat potato stew for all I care. So he takes me by surprise and sneaks in a swing at me. But he only got in the first punch before I laid him out flat …"

It's such a tall tale, I can't believe how the fellas seem to be lapping it up. Pete catches my glance. For just a second and only for me, his face lets show the truth of how his eye got blackened. Then he goes back to spinning his yarn for the boys. It seems that all of a sudden this town is full of nothing but secrets and lies. I leave him to it and head into the classroom.

At the end of the day, I tell John, Will, and Annie to head home without me. I'm waiting for Pete, who has been held back by Miss Carmichael for his poor showing on the grammar test she gave the senior grades today. I've got a question for Pete that needs to be asked in private. From the way he's been avoiding me all day, it seems he knows what that question is.

Just about everybody else has cleared off by the time he comes out of the schoolhouse. He pauses when he sees me sitting on the step, like he knows what's coming and he's not pleased about it.

"What are you still doing here, George?"

"How'd you get that shiner? And don't try telling me it was a drunken Irishman."

He walks ahead of me, his right eye turned away.

"Leave it be, George," he says. "It's none of your damn business."

I have to quicken my pace to match his gait, his legs being that much longer than mine. I still have a question to ask him.

"Pete, tell me again about seeing Louie Sam on the road from Lynden on the day Mr. Bell died."

Now he's looking at me full on. He's looking at me like I've lost my mind.

"I've told that story a hundred times," says Pete. "Are you stupid or something that you need me to tell it again?"

"Just tell me what you saw."

"I saw that redskin with murder in his eyes. The look on his face filled me with terror."

It strikes me that he uses the same turn of phrase every time he tells it, like he's reciting one of Mr. Shakespeare's sonnets.

"But he was just a kid," I say. "What was so frightening about him?"

"He was a savage. Ask General Custer what a savage is capable of."

"I saw Louie Sam with my own eyes, Pete. He was small—smaller than me even. And at least a head shorter than you."

"Are you calling me a coward?"

No, not a coward—but maybe a liar. Now comes the question I've been wanting to ask him all day.

"Pete, did you really see him? Or did your Uncle Bill tell you to say you did? Or your pa?"

Pete stops walking and glares at me. It's hard to tell if it's rage burning in his eyes, or fear.

"Are you some kind of police detective now, George?" he says. "Let me tell you what happens to police detectives around here."

"Tell me," I say.

His voice goes low.

"They get beat up and run out of town, counting themselves lucky to still be breathing as they go. So stop poking your nose where it doesn't belong."

So that's what Mr. Hopkins meant by Mr. Clark being persuaded to change his plans. I stand my ground.

"Answer my question. Did you see Louie Sam or not?"

"Yes! I saw him."

"Did he look the way you claim he did? Like a murderer?"

Pete hesitates. He's faltering.

"Pete," I say, "was he carrying a rifle with him when you saw him?"

He's moving his head from side to side like he's trying to shake something off, which is as much as admitting there was no rifle. He looks weighted down. He looks like he might be readying to unload the truth. Then of all things he lets out a laugh.

"Don't you get it, George? It doesn't matter. None of it matters."

"Yes it does," I tell him. "It matters if Louie Sam was innocent."

"Who does it matter to, except a bunch of government bigwigs who can't prove a thing?"

"It matters to his people," I say. "It matters to his family." And I realize how much it matters to me. "It isn't right that an innocent boy died to cover up somebody else's crime. Just tell me, Pete. Did somebody tell you what to say to Sheriff Leckie to make Louie Sam look guilty?"

He lets out a long sigh, like he's fed up with holding the truth inside him.

"Pa did," he says. "And if he ever finds out I told, he'll kill me."

Pete isn't laughing any more. Not one bit.

CHAPTER TWENTY-SIX

IN THE EARLY EVENING, John and Will are splitting wood while Annie helps Mam wash up from dinner. Mam is more like her old self again, relieved that Teddy is crying to be fed all the time. I have waited for a good moment to get Father alone. I find him down by the mill seated on a stump, enjoying his pipe on this fresh spring-like evening while looking out over the millpond. He's watching a pair of ducks swimming and diving. He turns and cocks an eye at the sound of my approach, as if to say that I'd better have a good reason for disturbing him.

"I have proof," I tell him.

"Proof of what?"

"That Louie Sam didn't do it. Mr. Harkness told Pete to lie to Sheriff Leckie about seeing him on the day Mr. Bell died."

"You mean he didn't see him?"

"He saw him all right. But all Louie Sam was doing was walking along the road minding his own business. He wasn't carrying a rifle. All that talk about

Louie Sam having murder in his eyes, that was pure invention coming from Mr. Harkness. I think he was in on Mr. Bell's murder, Father," I tell him. "Dave Harkness and Bill Osterman were in on it together."

Father draws on his pipe, looking out over the pond while he takes this in. He doesn't seem the least surprised.

"We have to do something," I tell him.

"Who said," he asks, as though he hasn't heard me, "'For every action there is an equal and opposite reaction'?"

Father is fond of testing me like this. I should know the answer, but at this moment I am too flummoxed to recall it. I hazard a guess.

"Charles Darwin?" I say, knowing that Father is a great admirer of the famous man of modern science.

He gives me a pitying look for my ignorance and tells me, "It was Newton."

I'm still not following him. What has Sir Isaac Newton got to do with Pete Harkness lying about Louie Sam? He gives his pipe a suck and lets go a long stream of smoke.

"Whatever action we take, George, we must think carefully about the reaction," he says.

So that's it. He's worried about what will happen if we take a stand against Mr. Osterman and Mr. Harkness. Never before have I felt the need to talk back to my Father as I do now. I remember the Bible passage, the one from Deuteronomy—about making amends.

"Those two spilled innocent blood, twice over," I say. "We have to make it right in the sight of the Lord, don't we? Like the Bible says."

Father casts me a look. He doesn't like my tone. He doesn't like being preached to.

"Explain yourself," he says sternly.

I do my best to stay calm and put my feelings into words.

"Louie Sam was just a boy," I tell him. "He had a mother, and people who mourn for him. He didn't deserve to die the way he did, alone and scared. He deserves justice, same as Mr. Bell does."

Father's watching me like a cat watches a trapped mouse he's going to devour any minute. But then I get the shock of my life.

"I can not argue with ye there, son," he says. "I can not argue with ye there."

He goes quiet. A wave of relief runs through me that he's not angry I spoke my mind, but it's more than that—it's a feeling of hope that maybe together we can set things right. I sit down on the grass beside him. The two of us watch the mallards dive and surface until it's almost dark. As we're walking back to the cabin together, at last he speaks.

"In the South, they'll string a white man up as a traitor for so much as believing that coloreds should be free."

"But slavery is over," I say. "Mr. Lincoln settled that."

"Aye," he replies, "and look what happened to him."

A Confederate shot Mr. Lincoln dead, that's what happened.

"There's no need to worry your mam about this business," says Father. "Let's keep it between us men."

"Yes, sir," I tell him, proud that he includes me as a man. But now I feel the weight of being a man, too.

WEDNESDAY MORNING FINDS Father and me seated side by side on the wagon bench with Mae and Ulysses trudging us toward town. It's a clear morning, but it rained overnight, making the track muddy and hard going. John, Will, and Annie are in the back. They're getting a treat—a ride to school instead of walking. But Father's and my destination is not the schoolhouse. We are heading to Sheriff Leckie's office. It is two weeks since we last saw him, when he met the posse on the Whatcom Trail on his way back from Canada. Two weeks since Sheriff Leckie witnessed the Canadian lawman take Louie Sam into custody, and since Louie Sam died. With the Canadian detective run out of town and everybody else too scared to speak the truth, Sheriff Leckie is our last hope.

The sheriff's office is at the far end of Nooksack Avenue. It was one of the first buildings they put up, back in the gold rush days of twenty years ago. From the look of it, it was thrown up in a hurry—really nothing more than a small square shack fancied up by a false clapboard front meant to make it look less paltry. Father and I wait outside in the wagon for nigh an hour before we see Sheriff Leckie coming down the boardwalk from the Nooksack Hotel, where he's probably been breakfasting.

We climb down from the wagon. Father shakes Sheriff Leckie's hand and introduces himself, and me—just in case the sheriff has forgotten us since that Sunday morning when we met over the body of Mr. Bell. But Sheriff Leckie remembers me just fine and praises me for my clear-headedness on that occasion.

"What can I help you fellas with this fine morning?" says the sheriff.

"May we talk inside?" Father asks, because even though there is barely a soul on the street at this hour, the business that brings us to talk to the sheriff is for his ears alone.

As we follow Sheriff Leckie inside the jail, he asks me how my arm got broken and I tell him. Inside, the first thing that hits me is the smell—like an old privy. The jail is sparsely furnished—just a desk, a wood stove, and one small cell with iron bars set in the door as a window. It looks like it hasn't been occupied in a long while. I'm guessing it got more use back in the gold rush days when there were lots of folks passing through hoping to make a fast dollar, be it from panning or pilfering. The sheriff sets about starting the wood stove, which I'm grateful for because it's cold and damp in here. The only chair in the room is the one behind the sheriff's desk, so Father and I must stand to say our piece.

"George has some information he'd like to pass along," says Father.

"About what?" asks the sheriff, stoking the fire he's got started in the belly of the stove.

"About the murder of James Bell."

At this the sheriff looks up.

"I already talked to your boy the morning of the murder, Mr. Gillies," says the sheriff. "I don't see what else he could have to add now."

Father tells him, "It's new information."

Sheriff Leckie closes the door on the stove, then takes his time crossing the room to his chair behind the desk. He reaches into a drawer and brings out some paper and a pencil.

"Well, George," he says to me, "what have you got to tell me about a murder that's already been solved?"

He sounds annoyed, but I stand my ground. It helps to have Father by my side.

"The wrong person was punished for Mr. Bell's murder, sir."

"That's quite a claim. What makes you believe that?"

"I found out some things about Louie Sam, the native boy."

The sheriff slams the desk drawer shut, like the very mention of Louie Sam is a vexation to him.

"I haven't forgotten who Louie Sam is, son. And it's not likely I'm going to with the governments of two nations breathing down my neck about him, from Governor Newell on up."

I tell him, "He didn't kill Mr. Bell."

"You'll forgive me if I beg to differ with you on that point."

Father pipes up in my defense. "Sheriff, you should listen to what George has to say."

"All right, son. I'm listening."

He's looking up at me from his chair and waiting. Wouldn't you know that my mind picks this moment to go blank? There's so much to tell. I don't know where to begin. Then all of a sudden it's spilling out of me so fast that my tongue can't keep up with my brain.

"What people said about Louie Sam was dead wrong. He wasn't carrying a rifle with him when he came into town that Sunday morning to meet with Mr. Osterman—so he couldn't have shot Mr. Bell—and he didn't have murder in his eyes on his way out of town, neither. People were just making up stories to make Louie Sam look guilty—"

"Whoa. Slow down," says the sheriff. "What people?"

"Bill Osterman," I tell him. "And Dave Harkness, too."

Sheriff Leckie moves forward in his chair, leaning his elbows heavily on the desk.

"These are serious accusations you're making, George. You better have something to back them up with. You ever heard of a little thing called slander?"

I catch myself. I have a vague idea of what slander is.

"It's when you say something bad about somebody."

"It's when you say something bad about somebody *that's a lie*," he corrects me.

"I'm not lying! It's the truth!"

Father quiets me with a look, then tells Sheriff Leckie, "George hasn't said anything about this in public, and he won't. That's why we've come to you."

"There's nothing I can do with a bunch of rumors. Give me facts. Give me witnesses. What exactly are you basing this on? What makes you so sure Louie Sam didn't have a rifle on him?"

"I can't say who told me," I tell him. "I promised I wouldn't."

Sheriff Leckie throws his pencil down on the desk.

"Well then why are you in here wasting my time? What do you expect me to do? Go out and arrest Bill Osterman because a bunch of Indians say he's the guilty one?"

"Yes," I tell him. "And you should arrest Dave Harkness, too. And Mrs. Bell."

"On what charges?"

"Murder!" I say. "I'm a witness."

Father shoots me a look of surprise. It wasn't part of our agreement that I would say so much, but I can't stop now. Sheriff Leckie narrows his eyes.

"Are you telling me that you saw Bill Osterman, Dave Harkness, and Annette Bell murder Jim Bell?"

"I didn't see them, but I heard Dave Harkness and Annette Bell talking with Mr. Moultray about it."

"George," says Father in a warning voice, but I won't stay silent.

"Mr. Harkness and Mrs. Bell as good as told Mr. Moultray that Mr. Osterman did it, and that they were in on it, too."

"Where did you hear this?"

"At their house, on Sunday night—after I broke my arm. I stayed there."

"What exactly did you hear?"

"Mr. Moultray asked Mr. Harkness and Mrs. Bell right out if they or Mr. Osterman had something to do with Mr. Bell's murder on account of Mr. Bell suing Mr. Harkness, and they didn't deny it."

"I can't go around arresting upstanding citizens of Whatcom County based on hearsay from a kid."

A thought occurs to me.

"But, Sheriff, you have to arrest Dave Harkness and Bill Osterman anyway!"

"What are you talking about?"

"Governor Newell said just last Friday that he's ordering that the leaders of the lynch mob be arrested."

He looks me straight in the eye.

"I don't know what you're talking about, son. Nobody knows who led that posse."

I'm flabbergasted. He's the sheriff, sworn to uphold the law. How can he be speaking such a lie?

"But … you were there," I say. "I saw you. You were talking with Mr. Osterman and Mr. Harkness that night. And Mr. Breckenridge and Mr. Moultray, too. And Mr. Hopkins. They were the leaders. Everybody knows that."

"What I saw was a group of men disguised in such a way that I can not be certain of their identities."

"But—"

Father takes hold of my good arm.

"Leave it, George."

"But Father—"

"I said leave it!"

Father guides me out into the street without so much as a good-bye to take leave of Sheriff Leckie. He keeps his eyes forward. His jaw is tight as he unhitches Ulysses and Mae from the post. I'm confused by what just happened, and by Father's angry silence.

"I'm not sorry for what I said," I tell him.

Now he looks at me. There's surprise in his eyes, and maybe even a little pride.

"I'm glad to hear it," he says. "It's not you that should be apologizing, son. It's not you."

CHAPTER TWENTY-SEVEN

FATHER POINTS MAE AND ULYSSES back the way we came and we head down Nooksack Avenue in the direction of home. As we pass the Nooksack Hotel, who should we see coming out the door onto the boardwalk but Mr. Moultray? Maybe he's been seeing Mr. Osterman in the telegraph office, or maybe he was breakfasting with Sheriff Leckie.

"A conspiracy of ruffians," Father calls it. "I wish to God I'd had the good sense to listen to your mam that night," he says. "I wish I'd had no part in their filthy business."

"There's others that feel the way we do," I reply. "There's Mr. and Mrs. Stevens. And Mrs. Thompson. Maybe Dr. Thompson, too," I add, although I haven't forgiven the doctor for giving up on Teddy the way he did.

Father says nothing. I can see he's thinking it over.

"We could get a message to Governor Newell," I go on. "We could write him a letter and tell him who the leaders of the posse were."

"Aye," he says, "but let's not fool ourselves. These are murderers. It's a dangerous business."

"Not if there's enough of us."

We've reached the edge of town. This is where Father should be stopping the wagon so that I can hop off and get to school, but he seems to have forgotten all about that, and I am not about to remind him.

"Perhaps I should pay Mr. Stevens a visit," he says.

The Stevenses' sawmill is right on our way, but Father reins Mae and Ulysses to a halt. He hasn't forgotten, after all.

"Off to school with ye," he tells me.

I jump down and he slaps the reins, calling to Mae and Ulysses to quicken their pace, like he can't wait to talk to Mr. Stevens. I'm heartened by the prospect of finding like-minded souls to band together in defiance of Bill Osterman and Dave Harkness.

I CAN HEAR MISS CARMICHAEL giving the morning lesson in mathematics to the senior class as I slip into the schoolhouse. She is not pleased with me for being late. I make my apologies and take my seat. Half listening to the lesson, I glance around the room at the seniors, boys and girls I've grown up with, wondering how many of their folks besides Abigail's might side with us. Tom Breckenridge's pa I know for sure stands with the posse leaders. There's Walter Hopkins, whose father, Bert, at the hotel

keeps warning me to keep my mouth shut—so it's a
fair bet that Mr. Hopkins won't be opening his own
mouth any time soon. Kitty Pratt's father was the one
who struck Louie Sam in the head with his rifle butt.
Under ordinary circumstances, Mr. Pratt is a nice man,
good with a story and with the fiddle. Maybe he looks
back on that night with regret. Maybe secretly he's
one of us.

By noon the day has turned warm. Miss Carmichael
makes us take our lunch buckets outside into the
sunshine. I see Kitty with Abigail, so I go over to
them. They're sitting on a bench with Mary Hecht,
who considers herself the queen bee even though she's
skinny and plain-looking compared to Abigail.

"Why were you late this morning?" Abigail asks.

"I had some business to attend to," I tell her.

"You're making yourself sound awful important,
George," remarks Mary.

"You certainly are," agrees Kitty, pulling a blond
braid through her fingers. "What kind of business
would that be?"

All three of them are staring at me waiting for an
answer. If it were just Abigail and Kitty, I'd tell them.
But Mary I'm not so sure of. I remember seeing her pa
that night, one of the pack. I have no idea where Mr.
Hecht might stand.

"Cat got your tongue?" snips Mary.

"Stop teasing him, Mary," Abigail tells her, getting up.

She takes me by my good arm and leads me away from them.

"You got to be more careful," Abigail tells me, keeping her voice low.

"They don't know what kind of business I'm talking about."

"George, everybody knows what kind of business! Walter Hopkins has been going around saying you went to the hotel yesterday to spill the beans to that detective."

I look over to Walter. He's standing at the edge of the schoolyard with Tom and Pete. Pete's at least a hand taller than either of the other boys. He lets out a big laugh at something Tom is saying.

"But I didn't talk to the detective," I tell Abigail. "He left town."

"It doesn't matter whether you talked to him or not. The damage is done."

"What damage?"

She purses her lips like she's afraid to say. She gives a nervous look over to where Kitty and Mary are watching us.

"We're not giving up," I tell her. "My father wants to call a meeting of the like-minded. We're going to send a letter to Governor Newell, telling him who the leaders of the posse were."

She gets a frightened look.

"Are you crazy?" she whispers.

"My father's going to talk to your father about it,"
I tell her. "We'll be okay if we stick together. Strength
in numbers."

"You told your pa about the rifle, didn't you?" she
says, still whispering. "You promised to keep that
secret!"

"All I told him was that your pa sides with us," I
tell her. She's making me mad. I want her to be better
than this. I want her to do what's right. "What's the
use in thinking the lynching was wrong if we're not
prepared to stand up and say so?"

She seems a little ashamed of herself at that. But
she's jumpy as a cat, glancing around at Mary and
Kitty, and over to Tom Breckenridge like she doesn't
want to be seen talking to me. I calm down and try for
her sake to appear like we're speaking normally and
not arguing.

"Do you think Kitty's pa might agree with us? Or
Mary's?" I say. "Can you ask them to tell their folks
about the letter?"

"I can't ask Mary," she replies. "She's so stuck on
Tom Breckenridge she agrees with every fool thing he
says. Kitty … maybe."

"It's the right thing to do," I tell her.

"You don't have to be so high and mighty about it,
George," she shoots back.

She's got some of her old spit back. For some
reason that makes me smile. And then she's smiling

back at me. We bend our heads together so people will think we're having sweet talk, when in fact we spend the remaining minutes of the lunch hour discussing who else might be persuaded to pass the message on to their parents. Ellen Wallace's father rode at the back of the posse—maybe that was because he had doubts about being there. Donny Erskine's pa wasn't there at all, due to his cow calving that night. But maybe that was just an excuse. Abigail says she'll talk to them, that it's safer for everybody if they're seen talking to her instead of me.

When we head back into the schoolroom after lunch, I get the feeling that Tom Breckenridge is keeping his eye on me.

AT HOME IN THE EVENING, once the younger children are in bed, Father says that Mr. Stevens agrees that something has to be done. He and Mrs. Stevens are willing to hold the meeting at their place, so including Mam that makes four voting citizens prepared to stand up and tell the truth. Mrs. Stevens believes Mrs. Thompson may be persuaded to join us, as well as Dr. Thompson.

"It can't hurt to have the town doctor on our side," says Mam, though something in her voice says she has no more forgiven him than I have.

"There may be others, too," I tell them. "Abigail is spreading the word."

"If we're to succeed," says Father, drawing on his pipe, "we must act swiftly and discreetly. We can't be sure of who we can trust."

The meeting has been set for tomorrow evening. Mam insists that Agnes and Joe be invited, too, but Father thinks it would be a mistake to invite the Indians. He says it's one thing to right a wrong that's been done to one of them, but quite another to start treating them like they have equal say with the settlers. As Indians, Agnes and Joe aren't voting citizens, anyway. John pipes up that he agrees with Mam about the Hamptons, but Father tells him to shush.

So we have a plan. Tomorrow night the right-thinking people of the Nooksack Valley will gather to sign a letter to Governor Newell asking that he order the arrest of Bill Osterman, Dave Harkness, Bill Moultray, Robert Breckenridge, and Bert Hopkins on the charge of leading the lynch mob that unlawfully hung Louie Sam.

CHAPTER TWENTY-EIGHT

I WAKE UP THURSDAY MORNING with my nerves on edge. I wish we could have the meeting right now instead of waiting for tonight. With all the enemies that homesteaders are used to facing, from wild animals to wild savages, it's a bad feeling to know that your worst enemies are right here among you, the very people you used to rely on to help stave off all those other enemies. And it's frightening to know that Bill Osterman and Dave Harkness are the sorts that won't think twice about taking somebody else's life if it'll make their own lives safer, richer, or more comfortable. In my view, the pair of them are double murderers. First they killed Mr. Bell, then they killed Louie Sam. Who pulled the trigger or yanked the rope tight isn't the point. The point is that those two men wanted the other two dead, and dead is how they managed to leave them.

Father seems in a fine mood when he heads out to the fields with John to start seeding the barley. He's like his old self, his own man again at last. But Mam

must be rattled like me, because she snaps at little
Teddy to hush when he cries from his cradle while
she's trying to make breakfast. That's the first time I've
heard Mam say a harsh word to the baby, so grateful
has she been that he's found his lungs and his appetite.
Gypsy starts barking at something out in the yard,
making us jumpier still. Then there comes a knock at
the door. We all feel uneasy at that knock. Who could
be coming to visit with the sun barely up?

"It's probably Agnes. Let her in, George," says
Mam, wiping her hands on her apron.

When I pull open the door, to my surprise there's
nobody there. Then I notice a horse hitched to the
post—Mr. Bell's horse, the one that Pete and I rode
when we followed the lynch mob north. A crazy
thought comes into my head, that maybe Mr. Bell's
ghost rode the horse here as a sign to show us we're
doing the right thing, avenging his murder. When
I step outside, I see just how foolish a notion that
is. Mrs. Bell is standing a few paces off, admiring a
dogwood bush that's started to blossom. She's wearing
the getup I saw her in when I mistook her for a man a
couple of weeks ago, outside the Nooksack Hotel—a
wide-rimmed hat and an oilskin coat. She gives me a
broad smile.

"George!" she says. "Just the fella I'm looking
to see."

Mam comes outside. So shocked is she at the sight

of Annette Bell on her stoop that she just stares at her saying nothing. The lack of welcome doesn't seem to trouble Mrs. Bell.

"Good morning, Mrs. Gillies," she says. "Fine morning, isn't it?"

"Yes, very fine," says Mam.

Her words are polite enough, but Mam's expression has gone cold and she makes no mention of inviting Mrs. Bell inside for a cup of tea and some breakfast, as she would any other passerby. If Mam's alarm bells are going off the way mine are, she's thinking it's an evil omen for Mrs. Bell to be showing up here now, what with the discussions we've been having about her and her dead husband.

"You're a long way from home, Mrs. Bell. What brings you this way so early?" asks Mam.

"I've come to see your George," she answers.

"What would you be wanting with my boy?"

Mam isn't sounding the least bit polite now. In fact, she sounds downright unfriendly. Mrs. Bell smiles, unperturbed.

"A word, is all. George is almost a grown man, Mrs. Gillies. Surely he needn't ask for his ma's permission to speak with the mother of one of his friends."

"Jimmy isn't my friend," I tell her.

It comes out ruder than I intended. Mrs. Bell gives me a look. She almost seems hurt.

"I meant Pete," she replies. My face must look

quizzical, because she adds, "Didn't Pete tell you? Mr. Harkness and I are to be married, as soon as all this unpleasantness settles down. So you see, I will soon be Pete's mother as well as Jimmy's."

Mam seems not to know what to say to that, nor do I. It's hard to know which is more scandalous—her living in sin with Mr. Harkness, or her marrying him so quick upon the murder of her other husband.

"George," says she, not waiting for us to find our tongues, "will you walk down toward the creek with me?"

Mam gives me a look that tells me not to go with her, but Mrs. Bell has put me on the spot saying that a man wouldn't let his mam tell him what to do. Besides, she seems all gentle and nice this morning. She starts down the path to our mill, and I follow her. She waits until we're well clear of the house before she starts talking.

"People are saying, George, that you overheard something you shouldn't have when you spent the night at my house this past Sunday."

So that's what this is about. My mind is working fast. Other than Pete, Sheriff Leckie is the only one I told about that. Which one of them spilled the beans? My panic must show, because she rests her hand on the cast on my broken arm to calm me.

"I like you, George. That's why I've come here. To save you from yourself."

"I don't understand," I say.

"Sometimes young men think they're being noble, when what they're really being is pig-headed. No good can come from going around spreading rumors about your neighbors, folks you might wind up living beside and doing business with for the rest of your life."

I have no idea what to say to that, but she doesn't seem to expect an answer. We've reached the mill house. She looks around and smiles at the pretty scene of the millpond. The water is smooth and calm and birds are chirping. She breathes in the fresh morning air.

"Some people," she tells me, "are angry at you for turning against your own kind."

I don't need to ask who those people might be. Her soon-to-be husband must be one of them, as well as Mr. Osterman and Sheriff Leckie.

"But I'm not angry with you, George," she says, "even though you have a funny way of showing your gratitude for us taking you in and feeding you and giving you a bed for the night when you were hurt so bad. I'm more *worried* for you, worried about what might befall a boy who doesn't know when to keep his gob shut."

She has lost all trace of gentleness. She looks me in the eye and tells me, "I see you have nothing to say, George. Best to keep it that way if you know what's good for you and your kin."

With that she heads back up the path to the house, taking long strides just like a man would. And I'm afraid of her, same as I would be if it were a man making threats against me and mine.

I GET BACK TO THE house in time to see the hindquarters of Mr. Bell's horse carrying Mrs. Bell down the path to the track. Mam is leaning over Teddy's cradle when I go inside. She keeps her back to me.

"What did that woman want with ye?" she asks.

I stop myself from telling Mam the truth. Mrs. Bell's threats would only put more strain on her shaky nerves, when she's just earned a respite by getting Teddy to fall asleep. Besides, Annie, Will, and Isabel are seated at the table eating their eggs and hotcakes. It's not proper for little kids to hear about how evil the human spirit can be.

"It's private," I tell Mam.

Mam turns and gives me a funny look.

"George Gillies, I'll not have you keeping secrets with the likes of her. Nor company, neither."

I feel myself blushing. I don't even want to think about what on earth she imagines is going on between me and Mrs. Bell.

"I got to get to school," I tell her, and I head for the door.

"You need to walk Annie and Will," Mam tells me.

"John's staying back to help Father with the planting today."

That would be my job, if my arm weren't broken. I feel as useless as a dull blade.

"I can walk Annie," says Will.

Mam looks at Will, and finds a smile for him.

"I'm forgetting how much you're grown," she tells him. To me she says, "I'll send your lunch with the children."

I TOLD MAM A WHITE LIE—I'm not going to school. I just need air. Outside, I think that maybe I should go find Father in the fields and tell him about Mrs. Bell's visit. But what exactly can I tell him, except that I let a woman scare the willies out of me? I need to go someplace where I can think. I start walking, and before I know it I'm at the creek. I keep walking along the creek, until the Hamptons' shack comes into view. Joe is outside, near their cook fire. Something tells me that Joe is exactly the one I need to talk to. Maybe that's why my feet have led me this way.

CHAPTER TWENTY-NINE

THE HAMPTON PLACE ISN'T neat and tidy like ours. There is no tilled garden waiting to be planted. The shack is surrounded by brambles. The walls are of logs and the roof of deer skin, making it look half Indian tepee and half a white man's cabin. The cooking fire is outside. A big cast iron pot is propped up over the red-hot embers with something that smells like porridge cooking in it. Joe has got a newly killed buck hanging from a tree branch. He's got the carcass split open and he's putting the guts into a bucket—so fresh they're steaming. He tells me to take a load off, so I take a seat on a stump of wood set up for that purpose near the fire.

"You were right about Louie Sam," I tell him. "I know he didn't shoot Mr. Bell."

"Did you come over here to tell me what I already know?"

I falter at that. Why did I come here? What is it I want from Joe? Maybe I want reminding that there's a wrong that must be righted, no matter how much risk it brings down on the heads of us Gillies. I find myself saying, "Some of the settlers are holding a meeting. We're sending a letter to the governor to tell him who led the lynch mob, so they'll be arrested and sent to Canada to face justice."

Joe finishes gutting the deer. He carries the bucket to the pot over the fire and, fishing out the kidneys and the liver and the heart, tosses them into it. He does all of this without speaking a word in response to what I've just told him. At last I say, "I thought you'd be happy to hear that."

"My cousin is still dead," says Joe. "But maybe you sleep better at night now, without him in your dreams, so that's good."

His voice isn't angry, but his words are. I feel bad that he thinks I'm fighting for justice just to make myself feel better, to ease my guilty conscience. Maybe that's why I find myself telling him what I have told no one else.

"I saw him on the telegraph trail, south of the river," I say. "He came to me."

When I say it out loud, it sounds crazy. But Joe doesn't seem to think so.

"What was he doing?"

"He was walking through the woods, alongside me. I was in rough shape at the time. I fell and broke my arm and I was all alone. It was a comfort to see him, even though I knew he had no cause to be friendly to me."

"Did he speak to you?"

"No. But I thought he was smiling."

"He was like that. He liked a good joke. He had a temper on him, too, though. Like his pa." Then he adds, glancing at my cast, "Maybe he was smiling because he saw your arm was broke."

That hadn't occurred to me before.

I ask, "You reckon it was really him?"

"You got to be careful with the spirit world," says Joe. "They don't like loose talk about them from the living. I heard about a man who told a missionary about the river spirit, and he wound up drowning."

That's no kind of answer—just superstition.

"That isn't a Christian way of looking at it," I tell him. "You can tell God anything. He knows everything."

Joe looks over at me across the fire. Now there's anger in his eyes.

"Does he know why the People of the River are dying?"

This takes me aback.

"What people?" I say. "Besides Louie Sam?"

He shakes his head.

"The whites brought sickness with them. Consumption. The pox. Whole families are dying, on both sides of the border. Ten years ago when the government tried to put the Nooksack on a reservation out by the bay, they came right back to the river, where they belong. Now … everything's changing. Settlers are stringing nets so the salmon can't get upstream. Fences are going up everywhere. I hunt for deer worrying I'll shoot somebody's cow instead and get strung up as a thief—on *our* land."

Their land. Their ways. I'd like to tell him that it's our land now, and that our ways are making a living and a future out of what was just wilderness. Still, I think about how Agnes knew better than Dr. Thompson—with all his learning—what to do for Teddy. I don't know what to say, so I wind up saying something dumb.

"Do you pray like we do?" I ask him.

He simmers down at that.

"Of course I pray," he says. "I prayed for this *mowitsh* to come and feed us."

So *mowitsh* means deer. That's what the Indian girl was saying to me about the twigs in my hair that day on the telegraph trail. Now I get the joke—she was saying the twigs made it look like I had antlers, like a deer.

"What are you smiling at?" says Joe. "You think praying is funny?"

"I don't mean offense, Joe," I tell him, serious again. "I reckon sometimes all we can do is pray."

I get to my feet, readying to take my leave, when Agnes comes out from the shack. She goes to the fire to give the cast iron pot a stir, nodding to me.

"Baby good?" she asks me.

"Teddy is good," I tell her. "Mam says he's like a little piglet grunting for his food."

"No *páht-lum*," she says.

"No, he's not drunk anymore. Thank you, Agnes. You saved him."

She straightens up and smiles at me. Reaching her hand up to my face, she pats my cheek like I'm a little kid, even though I'm a good foot taller than her. Her palm is tough as cowhide. Her eyes are sad and so tired they make *me* tired just looking into them.

"Where's your brother?" I ask Joe.

"Over at the residential school in Lynden. Learning to be white."

Agnes frowns at Joe and says something harsh to him in their language. He talks back to her. Whatever they're saying, I can tell this is an argument they've had before.

"What's she saying?" I ask Joe.

He laughs, "She's says I'm jealous because Billy knows how to read and write."

"I could teach you," I tell him. Joe gives me a cold look with those blue eyes, like he thinks I'm calling him stupid. "That is," I add, "if you ever wanted to learn."

He turns away and goes back to cleaning out the deer. Agnes sits down by the fire and stirs the pot. It seems neither one of them has anything left to say to me, or to each other.

"I guess I'll be going," I tell them.

252

Just as I'm on my way, Joe says, "The people will be glad to know there's whites who are sorry for what happened."

It's not much, but it's all the reassuring I'm going to get from him.

I WALK BACK ALONG the creek the way I came, thinking about my talk with Joe. There's a lot that's mysterious about the Indian way of thinking, and Joe is a particular curiosity. Sometimes he talks like a white man, and other times like an Indian. He'll always look like an Indian, though, except for his blue eyes, so I guess that decides the question as far as white folks are concerned. But it seems that everybody on this earth—whites and natives alike—suffers in one way or another. And, in one way or another, all of us are praying for that suffering to be eased.

CHAPTER THIRTY

I TAKE THE LONG WAY around the house so Mam
won't spy me and know that I am late for school again.
I walk swiftly along the path to town. Passing Mr.
Bell's burnt-out place, I give a thought to the stories
going around about Mr. Bell's ghost, and the hairs on
the back of my neck go up. I wish Joe Hampton had
been clearer with me about whether it was really the
spirit of Louie Sam that I saw walking last Sunday.

When I reach the schoolyard, the kids are already
outside having recess. I see Abigail sitting on the
bench with the other senior girls. I get the feeling she
sees me, too, though her head doesn't turn my way, or
even her eyes.

"What have you done now, George?"

I look down to see my sister Annie standing at my
elbow. Her hands are on her waist and her elbows are
sticking out.

"What are you talking about?" I say, cross that the
little snip of a thing is taking me to task like she's the
schoolma'am.

"None of the girls will even speak to me!"

"Well, maybe you should learn to talk more nicely to them then."

"It's not because of me. It's because of you! They won't say what you've done, but it must be something bad."

So word has spread about the meeting. Even the younger kids are fearful. I can't stop my glance from shooting over to Abigail, who's just ten paces away from me. Maybe she did too good a job letting people know. From the way she's coloring up, I know for certain she feels me looking at her, but she keeps her eyes forward on Mary Hecht, who's talking about a new dress or some such foolery. I look back to Annie.

"You need to trust in your own," I tell her.

And I mean it. Others may turn against me, but I won't stand for disloyal talk coming from my own sister. She lowers her eyes. When she looks up again, I see how afraid she is.

"What's going to happen, George?" she whispers.

"Nothing you need to worry about," I tell her. From the way she looks at me she knows I'm not telling her the truth.

Miss Carmichael comes out from the schoolhouse and rings the bell for us to come inside. As I climb the steps, Pete Harkness leans into me. There's snake venom in his eyes.

"You son of a bitch," he says. I can feel his breath

on my face. "What I told you was secret. So you go and tell the sheriff?"

"I didn't say where I heard it," I tell him.

"It don't matter," says he. "From this day forward, you and me are blood enemies."

He walks ahead into the school. So that's the way it is. Justice has cost me a friend.

AT THE END OF THE DAY I get a chance to talk to Abigail alone as we walk down the trail together toward her home and mine. She's quiet and on edge, like she doesn't know what to say to me.

"It seems you put the word around all right," I say.

It comes out like I'm accusing her of something, which isn't what I meant at all. She answers back angry, "I only talked to Kitty and Walter!"

I tell her, "Pete knows something."

"Well I sure as heck didn't tell him!"

"I didn't say you did."

"It sounds to me like you think so."

I stop in the middle of the track and turn to her. I'm so full of frustration, the way she's twisting everything I say.

"Abigail ..."

"*What?*"

The next thing I know, I'm kissing her. All of a moment, I understand what the fuss is about kissing—her lips are so soft and sweet-tasting. I don't want to stop, and it seems she doesn't want to, either. But then she pulls back from me, wiping the back of her hand across her mouth. Then I feel ashamed.

"Sorry ..."

"It's all right," she whispers.

In her eyes, I see she's as confused as I am. We start walking again. We go the rest of the way in silence. I want to take her hand, but I'm afraid it might scare her. So I walk by her side, feeling the pull of her. At last we reach the gate to her family's house and sawmill. She opens the gate and starts to go inside.

"Do you figure Pete knows about tonight's meeting?" I ask her.

"I don't know. I don't know who's telling what to who anymore."

"Your parents aren't going to back out, are they?"

"Of course they aren't. When my pa says he'll do something, he does it."

"Then I'll see you here tonight."

"I'll see you, George."

I walk the rest of the way home alone, trying to chase that kiss from my mind.

WE'RE QUIET AROUND THE table at dinner. Father and John are weary and hungry from their day in the fields. Annie picks at her food, her face full of worry— understanding in her own way that we are now a valley divided, that we Gillies are on one side, and most of her school friends' families are on the other. All of us, excepting Isabel and Teddy, are on edge about the meeting tonight.

John helps Father hitch Mae and Ulysses to the wagon. I do my best to tighten the harness with my one good hand. Father helps Mam, with Teddy in her arms, up to the bench. I climb into the flatbed. John, Will, Annie, and Isabel are all in the yard to wave us good-bye as we set out for the Stevenses' place.

The shadows are growing long across the trail, though we still have an hour of daylight ahead of us. Even Mae and Ulysses have got the jitters. When we pass Mr. Bell's place, Mae shies for no good reason and irks Ulysses, who nips at her. Father tightens the reins and speaks roughly to the two of them—which makes Teddy cry.

I can't stop myself from glimpsing through the bushes, even though what remains of the cabin is a sad and lonely sight, all the more so for the creepers and weeds that have already started to grow up around the charred timbers. It's like the wilderness can't wait to claim back Mr. Bell's stake for its own, like he never lived there at all. The forest makes me feel small. What if it does have a spirit, just like the Indians say? What if it's like that poet says? Nature is like God—always judging.

WHEN WE ARRIVE AT the Stevenses' house, we find a

single buggy hitched outside. It's Dr. Thompson's rig. The two fine bays that are harnessed to it are cropping new grass along the wagon track. Mismatched Mae and Ulysses look a sorry sight beside them. Father turns to me.

"Where are the others?"

"Maybe they're on their way," I say, hoping that at least one or two other settlers have yet to arrive—but I have a bad feeling.

Father helps Mam and the baby down from our wagon. I follow behind as they step up to the Stevenses' fancy porch. Abigail opens the door. She's been watching for us.

"They're in the parlor," she tells us in a rush—like she's got the jitters, too.

Their house is so fine that Father and I remove our muddy boots out on the porch before we follow Abigail inside. The parlor has heavy curtains around the window and furniture from back east, including a melodeon against one wall, its keys gleaming like the whitest teeth. Dr. Thompson and Mr. Stevens step forward to shake Father's hand as we enter. Mam is stiff when she says hello to Dr. Thompson. I can tell she isn't pleased to see him again, not after the damage he did to Teddy with his tonic. He chucks the baby under the chin with his finger without bothering to ask how it is that he is still alive. Teddy scrunches up his face and gives a little wail.

Mrs. Thompson is seated on a blue sofa that has feet carved in a curly pattern, like paws. She moves aside to make room for Mam, but I can see Mam's discomfort at sitting on such a fancy piece. Mrs. Thompson is nice. She makes Mam sit down and takes Teddy from her, admiring how much his color has improved. Never mind that it was her husband that gave Teddy up for dead. Abigail helps Mrs. Stevens bring in tea for everyone. I find a stool in the corner and sit down, mindful that Father has warned me to speak only when spoken to.

"It's a pity more citizens haven't joined us," Father says. "But we have six legal signatures amongst us. Mrs. Gillies has an excellent hand," he adds, making Mam blush, "if I may offer her services to copy down the letter we draft."

A look passes between Dr. Thompson and Mr. Stevens. Father sees it and asks, "I assume we are in basic agreement about what the letter should say?"

There's a tense feeling in the room. Neither man is in a hurry to speak, nor to look Father in the eye. At last Mr. Stevens breaks the silence.

"Mr. Gillies, the doctor has been persuading me that perhaps we are being too hasty about this letter."

Dr. Thompson speaks up.

"Here's the fact of the matter, Mr. Gillies. Consider what we stand to lose by acting against our own in such a rash manner."

"Our own?" says Father. "I'll have nothing to do with the likes of Bill Osterman and Dave Harkness, thank you very much."

"But the others—Bill Moultray and Robert Breckenridge and Bert Hopkins," pipes up Mr. Stevens. "These are good men. What's to become of Nooksack if they're taken away to some Canadian jail? And for what? A no-account savage."

I can't believe my ears. He sounds just like Annette Bell, telling Mr. Moultray that Louie Sam's life didn't count for anything, anyway, so it doesn't matter a whit whether or not the hanging was just.

"A life is a life!" I say.

Dr. Thompson glances my way, then tells Father, "I think it's best if your son waits outside."

"George is a witness," says Father, at the same time sending me a harsh look for my outburst. "He knows who murdered Mr. Bell, and it wasn't the Indian lad."

"Everybody knows who murdered him!"

It's Mrs. Stevens speaking up. Mr. Stevens tells her to shush, but the doctor's wife stands by her friend.

"Bertha states the plain truth," says Mrs. Thompson. "Dave Harkness and that woman put Bill Osterman up to shooting Mr. Bell."

"Mavis!" barks Dr. Thompson.

"The facts are the facts, my dear," she says calmly while rocking Teddy in her arms. "They're the only people who stood to gain from Mr. Bell's death.

Mr. Harkness and the Bell woman are now free to marry without fear of a lawsuit. And Mrs. Bell gets her hands on Mr. Bell's five hundred dollars, in trust for their son. Why Mr. Osterman went along with the scheme is beyond me, but he must have had his reasons."

"If we tar Osterman and Harkness, we tar Mr. Moultray, too—who's fighting for statehood, for growth and prosperity," says Mr. Stevens. "We need him. We can't afford to stay a backwater like we are now."

"Precisely," chimes in Dr. Thompson. "Who will settle here and buy Mr. Stevens's lumber without Mr. Moultray's wisdom and leadership?"

"So it comes down to greed against what's right," says Mam.

She's been so quiet, everyone's forgotten she's there. Now all eyes are upon her. The doctor puffs himself up with offense.

"Do not presume, Mrs. Gillies," he says, "to judge my moral character. As founding fathers of this town, it behoves the gentlemen present to consider what is best for all of us, for our future."

"Have you forgotten, Dr. Thompson," says Mam, "that we women have the vote now as well as the men, and a say in our future, too?"

"We shall see for how long, madam. We shall see for how long. This is proof of the unfitness of the weaker sex for political life!"

Father is angry at the tone he's taking with Mam.

"I'll not have you speaking to my wife that way!"

"Then control her, sir!"

Mr. Stevens steps in, speaking directly to Father.

"I'm sorry, Mr. Gillies. My wife and I can't sign your letter."

"And neither will Mrs. Thompson nor myself," adds the doctor.

I look over to Mrs. Stevens and Mrs. Thompson, so free with their thoughts a moment ago. Mrs. Thompson keeps her head bowed over Teddy. Mrs. Stevens busies herself pouring more tea. A terrible silence has fallen over the room.

"Very well then," says Father at last. "Anna, George—we're leaving."

Mam collects Teddy from Mrs. Thompson.

"Goodnight, Mrs. Gillies. He's a lovely baby," says Mrs. Thompson, as though nothing unpleasant has taken place.

I look over to Abigail, who's been standing in the doorway all this time, on the edge of the meeting. She meets my eyes with a pitiful look, from which I understand that she has no choice but to take her parents' side. She slips over to the far side of the parlor to give Father, Mam, and me a wide berth as we head to the door. Dr. Thompson is the only one to come out onto the porch after us.

"Gillies," he says to Father. "People in this valley

have worked hard for what they have, and they will punish those who act against them. I say this as a caution."

Father gives him no reply.

THE LIGHT HAS FADED to almost nothing as Mae and Ulysses lead the way home. The evening is so still, it's hard to say whether the hoot of an owl is coming from half a mile away, or five. Father's holding himself upright and stiff. After a long while riding, I say, "We can still write the letter."

Father crooks his neck toward me slightly. The tightness of his jaw matches that of his back and shoulders. He turns away again, saying nothing. It's Mam who speaks.

"Let it be, George."

Mae starts acting up, then Ulysses. Something has the pair of them spooked. Another moment or two, and I smell it, too—something burning. Father slaps the reins and with a shout makes Mae and Ulysses move forward. When we round a bend, we can see smoke rising above the trees in the direction of Sumas Creek—in the direction of our home.

CHAPTER THIRTY-ONE

WHEN FATHER SEES THE smoke, he stops the wagon and tells me to drive the rig the rest of the way home. I climb up front and take the reins while he jumps down and runs ahead, disappearing from our sight around the next bend. Mam clutches Teddy tight the whole rest of the way. It's not easy keeping Mae and Ulysses moving, me with only one good arm and they decided against forward motion. Finally, Ulysses stops and digs in his heels as only a mule can, refusing to go on no matter how much I holler at him. I get down and, taking hold of Mae's halter, lead her forward so that Ulysses has no choice but to follow.

When our cabin comes into sight, Mam and I are relieved to see it still standing, but we can see flames licking up over the trees in the direction of the creek. We can hear Gyp barking fiercely from down that way. Annie is out front with Isabel. They come running to meet us.

"The mill is on fire!" Annie calls to us.

"The mill is on fire!" says Isabel, Annie's echo.

Mam tells me to stop the wagon so she can get down. She puts Teddy into Annie's arms and tells her to take him and Isabel into the cabin and to keep them there.

"Where are John and Will?" she wants to know.

"Down at the mill with Father."

Mam starts running down the path to the mill. I tie off Mae and Ulysses to a tree and follow Mam, lickety-split. At the end of the path I find Mam stopped, staring at the wall of the mill, now a wall of flame—the roaring heat warping the air around it. Gypsy is at Mam's side, whimpering in between barks. Mam cries out, "How could they do such a thing?"

I look at the angry blaze and know in my heart that Mam is right—this is what Dr. Thompson meant when he talked about punishment. Through the smoke, I make out John and Will by the pond, scooping up buckets of water.

"Go back to the house, Mam," I tell her. "Take Gyp. Keep the children safe."

In a flash Mam sees what I'm driving at, that if they hate us so much they could set the mill on fire, they could do the same to our home. She calls to Gyp and hurries back up the path, while I run to the pond and grab a bucket to help John and Will haul water.

"When did it start?" I call to the boys over the din of fire and crashing timbers.

"'Bout half an hour ago!" shouts John. "Gyp was

barking and wouldn't stop. I came outside and smelled the smoke."

I turn to the mill with my full bucket and see Will handing off a pail to Father, who throws water at the east wall, the one containing the waterwheel. My heart takes a leap to see Joe Hampton at his side—I'm thinking that maybe with all of these hands we have a chance at saving something. I hand my water off to Joe, who pivots and splashes it onto a spur of orange and yellow that's making its way toward the wheel, which so far has been spared. He shirks off the blanket he's wearing as a poncho and tosses it to me.

"Get it wet!" he yells.

I leave the water buckets to John and Will and throw the blanket into the pond, finding enough strength in my left hand that between it and my good right one I can pull its sodden weight back out of the water. I carry it back to Joe, who grabs it and starts beating back the flames with it. I pick up my bucket and fetch more water. Father has three of us bringing him buckets now and is able to pick up the pace of dousing near the waterwheel while Joe works his way around to the south wall, where the flames are so fierce. So far the fire hasn't reached the creek-side north wall. If we can stop it from spreading any further, we'll keep the wheel from burning.

John and I are at the pond, side by side, filling our buckets when a gunshot cracks the air. We both look in the direction of our cabin where it came from, both with new fears. I glance over to Father and Joe, still working. Neither of them heard it. They're too close to the roar of the fire.

"You stay," I tell John.

I set down my bucketful of water so he can carry two, and I run up the path to our house. Mam is standing outside, holding Father's rifle. So that's where the shot came from. She calls to me, "There's two of them!"

I look to where I can hear Gyp barking, in the bushes along the track that leads to the house, and I see two points of light bobbing between the trees. Lanterns. Gypsy is out there, barking fiercely. I take the rifle from Mam and tell her to get back inside and lock the door. With only one good arm, I can't load the rifle—there's naught I can do but use it for show. But it's better than facing whoever's out there bare-handed.

There's a yelp from Gyp, and then she's silent. I don't see the lights from the lanterns any longer. I listen for the snap of a twig, but all is still. Mae gives a nervous whinny from where she and Ulysses are tied along the track. In the moonlight I can see her nodding and shaking her head. I step softly over to the wagon and use it for cover as I scan into the woods for movement, but there's none that I can see. I'm worried about Gyp, that she's gone so quiet. What have they done to her?

"Get off our land!" I yell. "I've got a gun!"

There's a choked off laugh, coming from the right of me—not far into the bush. It sounds like a kid!

"I can hear you!" I call. "I know you're there!"

A voice comes back at me, a voice I recognize as belonging to Tom Breckenridge.

"And what the hell are you going to do about it with one arm broke!" he shouts, taunting me.

"I know that's you, Tom!" I say.

Now I can see his lantern light through the trees, and I can hear the swish of undergrowth as he comes my way. There's a second light behind him, bobbing toward me.

"Who's with you?" I call.

But in another second I can see for myself. It's Pete Harkness.

"Unless you're planning on throwing that rifle at us, you may as well put it away, George," says Tom with a grin. "We know you can't shoot straight."

Tom looks over to Pete to see if he appreciates his joke. Pete gives a laugh. I lower the gun. I couldn't shoot them, even if it was loaded.

"Did you set the fire?" I say.

"What fire?" says Tom, still with that grin on his face.

"I'm telling the sheriff it was you!"

"Go ahead," says Pete, "if you think the sheriff's ever going to listen to you again after all the lies you've been telling him about folks."

"It's a shame about your mill," Tom says. "I hope nothing else bad happens to you." He turns to Pete. "C'mon," he says. "There's a bad smell around here, like dirty Indians."

"Or dirty Indian lovers."

"Same thing."

Tom and Pete step out of the bush and amble away toward the trail, like they're out for an evening stroll.

"Pete!" I call. Tom keeps walking, but Pete turns back to me. "What did you do to Gypsy?"

In the light from his lantern, I can see him lose his cocky look. For a second I see the old Pete, my friend. He knew Gyp from when she was a pup. When we were boys, we used to take our dogs with us when we went hunting for rabbits and the like.

"It weren't me," he says. For a second he seems broken up, then in a flash he gets angry. "You were there that night, George," he tells me. "It was your idea to follow them. You were part of it. Don't make like you wasn't."

I stare at him wishing with all my might that I could find some reason why he's wrong, why he had more to do with the lynching than I did, why he's guilty of taking a boy's life and I'm innocent. But he speaks the truth. I've got blood on my hands, same as him. The only difference between us is that I'm sorry for what happened. What use is that to Louie Sam?

Pete looks like he wants to say something more, but instead he just shrugs and follows Tom off down the track. I watch them go. There's no point in pretending there's something I can do about them. There's no point at all.

CHAPTER THIRTY-TWO

FOR THE REST OF THAT NIGHT I helped Father, Joe, and my brothers save what we could of the mill. The waterwheel wasn't too badly damaged, though the driveshaft was burned. Father thought about replacing it, but then he thought about how much business the mill was likely to see, given how the mood in the valley had swung against us. So the mill sits there as we left it that night, the east and creek-side walls mostly still standing, but the insides charred and in ruins.

At first light I went looking for Gypsy. I found her lying on her side behind a moss-covered log, the fur around her neck sticky with dried blood. Her throat had been cut by Tom Breckenridge. I knew we should count ourselves lucky that it was only the dog that died that night, and not one of the family, but I cried anyway—for Gypsy, for Louie Sam, and for the wrong I was part of and knew then I would never be able to put right, not with the whole Nooksack Valley bent on whitewashing the business of who really murdered James Bell.

For the next few months we heard rumblings about the Canadian government trying to find out who led the lynch mob, but Governor Newell stopped being governor in July, and the new governor, Mr. Squire, didn't take the same interest. Joe Hampton told me that most of Louie Sam's people, the Sumas, moved away from Sumas Prairie up the Fraser Valley while they waited for justice—because they felt safer farther away from the International Border.

After a while, people around Nooksack acted like they'd forgotten all about Mr. Bell and Louie Sam—mostly because neither was a subject for polite conversation, or any other kind of conversation, for that matter. Bill Moultray, Robert Breckenridge, Bert Hopkins, Dave Harkness, and Bill Osterman have gone on with their lives like nothing bad happened at all. So my guess is that the Sumas will be waiting for quite a while before they get the justice they expect for Louie Sam.

Late in the spring, Dave Harkness married Mrs. Bell, making an honest woman out of her—more or less. Mr. Moultray held a dance above the livery stable to celebrate the occasion. I hear that Kitty's father, Mr. Pratt, played his fiddle. We Gillies were not invited, not that I wanted to set foot near a Harkness ever again after what happened, nor near their kin Bill Osterman. Abigail stayed home that evening, too, even though she loves to dance. When she found out what

Pete and Tom did to our mill and to Gypsy, she would have nothing to do with them. I'm happy to say that at least Abigail is still my friend. Well, more than my friend. I guess you would call us sweethearts.

Agnes has gone back to live with the Nooksack. As for Joe, he talks about clearing the land around their shack and becoming a farmer. Then in the next breath he says he thinks he'll cross the border into Canada and go live in the wilderness, trapping and hunting like his mother's people have done for centuries. If he leaves, we'll miss him. We Gillies will never forget how he came to help put out the fire.

Once in a while, if I'm walking through the woods alone, I wonder if Louie Sam's spirit might come to me again. Joe says he could come as a raven or as a coyote, you never know. I've thought a lot about what I'd say to him this time if I had the chance. I'd tell him that I thought he was brave the way he held his chin up that night with all those grown men shouting at him and calling him names. I'd tell him that I'm sorry that I believed so quickly the lie that Bill Osterman made up about him. And I'd tell him that I pray for him to God, and to all the spirits of this valley.

AFTERWORD

THIS BOOK IS A WORK of fiction, but the key people and events are based on fact. On the evening of February 27, 1884, teenagers George Gillies and Pete Harkness secretly followed the Nooksack lynch mob as they traveled north into Canada with the aim of seizing Louie Sam for the murder of Nooksack resident James Bell, four days earlier. The mob, disguised in "war paint" and costumes, was led by William Osterman, William Moultray, Robert Breckenridge, and Bert Hopkins. Near the International Border between the Washington Territory and British Columbia, the lynch mob encountered Whatcom County Sheriff Stuart Leckie on his return from Canada, where that day he had witnessed Canadian Justice of the Peace William Campbell handcuff fourteen-year-old Louie Sam and leave him in custody overnight at the farmhouse of Thomas York, whom Campbell had deputized as a constable. The lynch mob sent one of their number ahead to Mr. York's farmhouse to pose as a traveler in need of a bed for the night. Mrs. Phoebe Campbell—Mr. York's daughter and the wife of Justice Campbell—later recounted that Mr. York believed that this infiltrator unlocked the farmhouse door after the household had retired for the night, thereby allowing the mob easy access to Louie Sam.

George and Pete were in Mr. York's yard when the mob entered his house and hauled Louie Sam, still handcuffed, outside. And they were present when, on the ride back south to Nooksack, the mob stopped just short of the border and put a noose around Louie Sam's neck. Eyewitness accounts report that when Louie Sam recognized William Moultray through his disguise, he spoke his only words of the night, recorded variously as: "Bill Moultray, I get you" and "I know you Bill Moultray, and when I get out of this I will get you." His identity exposed, Moultray slapped the flank of the pony that was carrying Louie Sam, causing the pony to bolt—and Louie Sam to hang.

It was never proven that William Osterman, the Nooksack telegraph operator, murdered James Bell. However, the historical record shows that immediately following Louie Sam's death the Stó:lō Nation presented evidence to the Canadian authorities that he was guilty, based on Louie Sam's account of his visit to Nooksack to seek work from Osterman on the morning of James Bell's murder. The Stó:lō were convinced that William Osterman lured Louie Sam to Nooksack as a scapegoat for the murder he planned to commit.

No clear motive existed for Osterman to murder Bell, apart from Osterman's friendship with his brother-in-law, Dave Harkness. But Dave Harkness and Annette Bell had plenty of motive. It was rumored that at the time of his murder James Bell was threatening to sue Dave Harkness and Annette Bell. Annette Bell inherited five hundred dollars from Bell in trust for their son as well as six hundred dollars in proceeds from the sale of his land—which the Harknesses used to open a dry goods store. Bill Osterman got the job of appraiser of Mr. Bell's estate, and so took his cut of the proceeds. Dave Harkness died the next year, in 1885. Annette Harkness continued to operate the dry goods store and the ferry at The Crossing after his death. In the Whatcom County census of 1885, she is listed as a merchant. She later married Dave Harkness's friend Jack Simpson.

The Washington Territory achieved statehood in 1889. Bill Moultray was elected to the first state senate and remained in that office for many years. It is true that women were given the right to vote in the Washington Territory in 1883, but in 1887 female suffrage was struck down by a ruling of the Territorial Supreme Court. Women would not regain the right to vote in Washington State until 1910, and federally not until 1920.

Records show that George Gillies was born in England and immigrated to the Washington Territory with his Scots-born parents, Peter and Anna, probably in the 1870s, where Peter Gillies built a gristmill on Sumas Creek. According to an interview published in 1946 that the then elderly George Gillies gave to the *Abbotsford, Sumas and Matsqui News*, he and his brothers discovered the body of James Bell on the morning of February 24, 1884, while on their way to Sunday school. However, the character of George Gillies as portrayed in this book is invented. I have taken creative license with George's redemptive arc and his slow dawning of awareness of the injustice committed against Louie Sam, and with the persecution that his family suffered as a result.

Fearing a cross-border war between the Stó:lō Nation and the American settlers, the B.C. and Canadian governments promised the Stó:lō swift action immediately following the lynching. Within two weeks of Louie Sam's death, Canadian authorities dispatched two detectives to the Nooksack Valley to identify the leaders of the mob. One of the agents, a Mr. Clark, was driven out after being threatened by Annette Bell with "catching an incurable throat disease." Prior to retreating to B.C., Agent Clark interviewed several Nooksack Valley residents who believed that motive and circumstances pointed to William Osterman as the murderer of James Bell. There was widespread belief that Louie Sam was framed by Osterman, who subsequently led the lynch mob in order to silence his scapegoat before Louie Sam could reveal the truth in a Canadian court of law.

Ultimately, neither Canadian nor American

authorities had the resolve to see justice achieved. After initial promises to the government of Sir John A. Macdonald in Ottawa to further the investigation, American interest fell off. Wrote Washington Territory Governor Newell in July, 1884:

> *It is well nigh impossible to make discoveries of a band of disguised people who, with the entire community, are interested in the secrecy which pertains to such illegal and violent transactions.*

In other words, despite the fact that the identities of the mob leaders were common knowledge, the American authorities had closed ranks with the settlers of the Nooksack Valley. It was left to Canada to initiate extradition proceedings, but the government did not act on the evidence gathered by Mr. Clark for fear of jeopardizing relations with the United States.

Within a few years, the Stó:lō population in the Fraser Valley declined due to the toll of European diseases. The influx of settlers further shifted the population ratio so that the Stó:lō became the minority in their own land. With the fear of an Indian uprising diminished by this decline in population, the Canadian government gave up its pursuit of justice for Louie Sam.

But the murder of Louie Sam remained an open

wound for the Stó:lō Nation. In 2006, healing began when the Washington State legislature approved a resolution expressing sympathy to the Stó:lō for the lynching, acknowledging that both Washington and B.C. "failed to take adequate action to identify the true culprit of the murder and bring the organizers and members of the lynch mob to justice." It wasn't a formal apology, but it was a recognition of Louie Sam's innocence.

Apart from recounting the horrors of the actual lynching, I found the most difficult aspect of writing this novel was presenting a truthful portrayal of nineteenth-century racism. Native Americans fell into a category all their own in the nineteenth-century pecking order of bigotry that targeted, among others, African-Americans, the Chinese, and the Irish. Native Americans were feared and reviled by many, especially settlers in the west, as hostile savages. They were romanticized by others as primitive children living in a natural, pre-civilized state. Missionaries saw the aboriginal peoples as heathens in need of Christian salvation and stepped up to the task—undermining First Nations cultures and languages and helping to spread European diseases like smallpox, tuberculosis, mumps, and measles that decimated aboriginal populations throughout North America.

Happily, today the Stó:lō Nation represents a thriving community of eleven bands—among them the Sumas—working toward self-government and the preservation of Stó:lō culture. It is my understanding that, to this day, the memory of Louie Sam remains very much alive in Stó:lō culture as an important reminder of the historical racism, injustice, and loss suffered by The People of the River.

—*Elizabeth Stewart*

PUBLISHER'S ACKNOWLEDGMENT

Annick Press wishes to acknowledge Stephen Osborne's powerful article "Stories of a Lynching," about the true events surrounding the lynching of Louie Sam, which appeared in issue 60 of *Geist* magazine. The revelations in this article were the motivating force for pursuing the story in a form that would appeal to young adult readers.

ABOUT THE AUTHOR

ELIZABETH STEWART HAS BEEN a screenwriter for twenty years. She has won several awards for her work on television series for young people, including *The Adventures of Shirley Holmes* and *Guinevere Jones*. She has also written movies for television, among them *Tagged: The Jonathan Wamback Story*, an examination of teen violence based on a true incident, and *Luna: Spirit of the Whale*, which chronicled the transformational effect of a stray killer whale on a First Nations community on Vancouver Island. Both of these films were nominated for Gemini Awards.

Elizabeth lives in Vancouver, British Columbia.

MORE AWARD-WINNING BOOKS FROM ANNICK PRESS

CHANDA'S SECRETS
by Allan Stratton
paperback $11.95 | hardcover $19.95
★ *Michael L. Printz Honor Book for Excellence in YA Literature, ALA*
★ *Top 10 Black History Books for Youth, Booklist*

Chanda, an astonishingly perceptive 16-year-old girl living in the small city of Bonang in Africa, must confront the undercurrents of shame and stigma associated with HIV/AIDS.

"No-one can read Chanda's Secrets and remain untouched by the young people who are caught in the AIDS pandemic and still battling to make sense of their lives."—Stephen Lewis, UN special envoy for HIV/AIDS in Africa

THE APPRENTICE'S MASTERPIECE: A STORY OF MEDIEVAL SPAIN
by Melanie Little
paperback $12.95 | hardcover $19.95
★ *Independent Publisher Book Award*
★ *White Ravens Collection, International Youth Library, Munich*

A brilliant and elegantly written story in verse about one of the most politically complex and troubling times in human history—the Spanish Inquisition.

"The subject and the history are enthralling ..."—Booklist

"This riveting story is peopled by flesh-and-blood characters and replete with ... historical detail."—School Library Journal

THE BITE OF THE MANGO
by Mariatu Kamara with Susan McClelland
paperback $12.95 | hardcover $24.95
★ *White Ravens Collection, International Youth Library, Munich*
★ *Silver Award Winner, Book of the Year, ForeWord Reviews*

The astounding true story of one girl's journey from war victim to UNICEF Special Representative.

"... a powerful commentary on one of the many costs of wars. An essential purchase ..."—Kirkus, starred review

"... this book will unsettle readers—and then inspire them ..."
—Publishers Weekly, starred review

CRY OF THE GIRAFFE: BASED ON A TRUE STORY
by Judie Oron
paperback $12.95 | hardcover $21.95
★ *2011 USBBY Outstanding International Books Honor List*

A girl's harrowing trek from exile and slavery to hope in a new land, based on the true experiences of a 15-year-old Ethiopian Jewish refugee.

"... shows with brutal, unflinching detail the horrors of refugee life and child slavery and the shocking vulnerability of young females in the developing world ..."—Booklist Online

THE HANGMAN IN THE MIRROR
by Kate Cayley
paperback $12.95 | hardcover $21.95

In 18th-century North America, a strong-willed 16-year-old maid caught stealing from her mistress must use her wits to escape death by hanging. Based on a true story.

"… does everything good historical fiction should—give the reader a tremendously detailed sense of time and place … through the eyes of a protagonist whose emotions are relatable to a modern audience."
—ForeWord Reviews

GENERALS DIE IN BED: A STORY FROM THE TRENCHES
by Charles Yale Harrison
hardcover $9.95

Drawing on his own experiences in the First World War, Charles Yale Harrison tells a stark and poignant story of a young man sent to fight on the Western Front.

"The best novel about Canadians in the Great War."—Professor J.L. Granatstein, former director, Canadian War Museum

"This is a powerful literary work that deserves an audience beyond young adults."—ForeWord Reviews